LOOKING FOR A GOOD DRAGON

A FATED MATES DRAGON SHIFTER NOVEL

MICHELLE ZIEGLER

Hearth Publishing

INTRODUCTION

All Irene wanted was freedom. What she got was an overprotective dragon and a crash course in men.

Irene did it. She finally got away from her fathers clutches and his evil minions.

She's not looking for a happily ever after—all she wants is to stay under the radar and make it on her own. She's even got herself a job, as a waitress in a strip club.

The tall, dark, and serious shifter in the corner has her on edge, though. Not because he scares her, but because her body seems to want him regardless of what her head says.

And sexy dragon shifters aren't anywhere close to under the radar.

It's only a matter of time before daddy-dearest finds her, and if this dragon wants to keep her, he'll need to prove to her that his skills are stronger than a panty melting kiss.

He's going to have to battle her past demons and protect her from the one man who could ruin it all.

Publisher's Note: This is a work of fiction. Names, character, places, and incidents are a product of the author's imagination. Locales and public names are sometimes used for atmospheric purposes. Any resemblance to actual people, living, or dead, or to businesses, companies, events, institutions, or locales is completely coincidental.

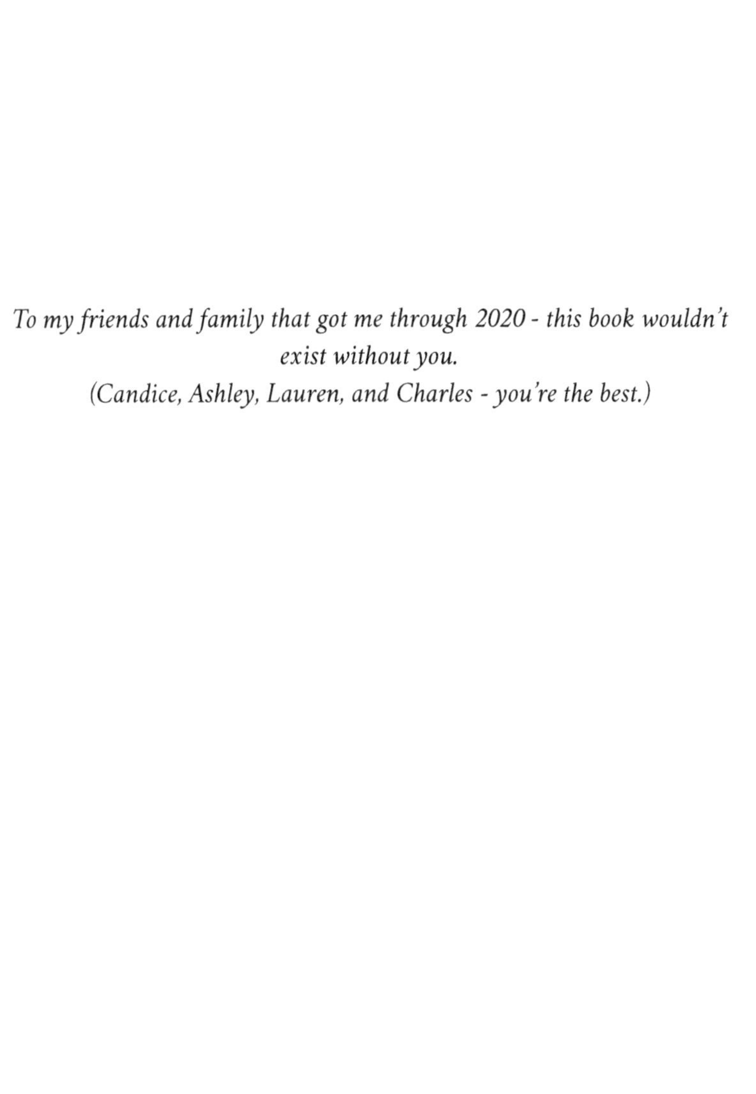

To my friends and family that got me through 2020 - this book wouldn't exist without you.
(Candice, Ashley, Lauren, and Charles - you're the best.)

ACKNOWLEDGMENTS

In the wake of 2020 and the pandemic we've all struggled. Thank you to my fans for begging for more and helping me see that reading has helped them escape the crazy.

Thanks to my husband for the support to get this book done! Without him listening and also taking the kids I wouldn't have given Irene her fair chance to tell her story.

I have so many readers to thank, but especially my Beta/Alpha readers and my proofreader.

Lucia, Bev, Carol, Donise

You guys are without a doubt my sanity!

Thank you Emcat Designs for my cover.

Of course, my review team is a group that has my undying gratitude!

AND ALWAYS! Thank you readers! Thank you for giving me a chance and escaping into my world and loving some confused dragon shifters from outer space. Thank you for following me this far into this crazy adventure.

Come join me on the journey inbetween the pages. Join my Newsletter: http://michellezieglerauthor.com/contact/

"Remove your hand before I rip it off your body," Irene whispered-yelled over the music. His glazed over eyes said he didn't understand through the alcohol induced stupor. They needed a better bouncer. Where was that asshat, anyway?

She looked around, grabbing the wandering hand of another drunk customer. Her life wasn't glamorous, but at least it was hers. Finally.

"Shit. Ouch. Damn woman."

Mr. Handsy released her ass.

"Just because it's on display doesn't mean it's yours."

"Everything okay, Ivy?" asked a brick wall of a man. Unfortunately, his IQ matched.

"Yeah, thanks. Maybe you could try to be a little more observant Burt?"

He nodded and grabbed up the sleazy man by the scruff of his shirt.

"Cab's out front. You can leave now."

"Fuck, man. Fine. If she doesn't want someone grabbing her shit, maybe she shouldn't fucking look like a hooker."

Irene lost her patience. One too many nights sick and tired of being manhandled, grabbed, and ignored. She didn't mind the grabbing. She minded being ignored. If she wanted to be ignored she'd have stayed in that hell of a lab with her father. A shiver ran the length of her spine. No. She'd never go back, and that's why she hid in the last place he'd ever look for her.

The music thrummed as a new dancer took the stage. Irene grabbed the glasses off the table, ignoring the swirl of lights. This place had taken some getting used to. She'd gone from a stark white, sterile environment where no one talked much to an environment where there was constant noise and scents she didn't know existed.

"Hey, Ivy. Table six," the bartender, Trent, yelled.

She rolled her eyes and headed for whoever had just come in. And that's how the night would go. Table after table. Cleaning up, keeping the drinks flowing, teasing them until the actual girls they wanted strutted their stuff up on stage or those that came around to tease these delusional and desperate men. Here though, she was Ivy, a girl from the streets with a questionable past that no one gave two craps about.

Here she was Ivy, a down on her luck homeless chick. Not Irene, a girl who had seen more evil for three lifetimes.

At night, when she tried to find sleep between the nightmares and memories, she relished the fact no one cared about her backstory. The marks on her arms? Easily covered with tattoos as she'd quickly found out. No one had to know that her life had been hell and that even here, nearly naked, serving depraved men their drinks was still an improvement.

She'd be happy to let them forget about their own personal hells, because she was desperate to forget her own.

If only everything from her past would disappear. The tingles that seemed to dance along her skin reminded her she wasn't alone. A quick glance over her shoulder and the shadow in the corner brought her some form of comfort and also fear.

She dropped her head to the floor. She just had to keep her

head down. Forget about the shadow and forget about the past. She even ignored the girls that took men in the back, even if every part of her wanted to throat punch those men. This was their choice, the woman's. Not the men's. Here, the women were in charge. She'd clarified that she would not dance, and she wasn't the kind to give the extra special anything and that had been okay.

She was allowed to say no, for the first time in her life.

She glanced over her shoulder again. Shadow was still there. Huge, menacing, and hot. The strength radiating off of him made her want to know if what she remembered was real. If what she could remember through her haze of withdrawal was real. Her father's meds seemed to be out of her system, finally. She hoped.

Irene moved about the club, lost in her world. She caught the bright red of Ruby-Red's hair from across the club. You couldn't miss that woman. She was eccentric, but she also didn't question Irene's digging in dumpsters or sleeping under her stairs. Looking around at the topless dancer and a few men belly up to the stage, she still appreciated that Ruby felt a calling to help women down on their luck.

Irene hadn't cared, or rather she still didn't care. She was numb.

Or almost numb.

Too many sleepless nights for her to decide what she was. Her skin itched, and she knew he watched her. Her dreams were haunted by purple glowing eyes. The ones from her dragon.

No, not her's. She'd walked away. That night came back to her as if it were yesterday. She absently wiped a table, fighting against the tightness in her chest. Even now, the feeling of drowning was fresh in her mind. The moment she walked away from him she felt off.

She still didn't know why she'd done it. Maybe it had been the panic or possibly the drugs in her system from her father, but whatever it was had her jumping off his back feet above the ground. A floodgate of emotion had cracked the day she'd touched him, the dragon. All her walls had flexed and cracked. She'd nearly drown in emotions she'd worked so hard to shut off.

Even now, as he stood in that corner where she could feel his presence, she couldn't understand why. She'd begged him to leave her. Screamed at him. Somehow, though, he was still here.

"Ivy, another," called Trent from the bar.

She tried to shake away the constant wave of new and more confusing feelings and thoughts.

"Thanks, Trent."

She ignored the fact the corset top pinched her chest as it barely held her in. Fuck, like it wasn't hard enough to breathe without something trying to strangle her.

Her sister had found someone. If she could find happiness, why couldn't Irene.

She shuddered at memories that never went away. The cries of too many suffering souls. Bile rose in her throat.

"Another shot," she said, trying to swallow down the pain.

"You good Ivy?" asked the bartender. She nodded. She couldn't speak past the squeezing panic in her throat.

She was the devil's daughter. She stood by and watched, no she stood by and waited for the opportunity to relieve them of their lives. The moment her father left, she used the only tool she had. The curse her father had never seen. Where her sister couldn't hide, Irene did so with expertise.

What if she could be happy, though? What if it was with her rescuer?

Trent smiled at her. "Sure. Are you really doing okay? You seem more spacey than normal."

Irene blushed. If he only knew that she was obsessively thinking of a stranger, a dragon no less. Her body seemed on board though, and she pressed her legs together.

"I'm fine. Just fine. The night's almost over. It will be fine."

He looked at her funny. "Okay. If you say so, kid."

Irene pursed her lips. Kid? Whatever. She wasn't here to make friends. She wasn't here to daydream about a dragon either. No. She was here to hide and live out her life without being a lab rat.

Irene scratched at her forearm out of habit. The chemicals her father's scientists had injected burned, and she still had a hard time forgetting. She dropped off the drink and as she turned around caught the flash of purple.

Did she want him to approach or just leave? Why couldn't she remember more from when he'd brought her here?

Oh, right? The fever. The pain of poison running through her veins was too strong for logic and stronger than even the emotions trying to remind her she was still alive and still partially human.

She remembered enough, but not everything.

The heat of his skin under her fists as she'd beat against his solid chest. His words hadn't made any sense. He'd tried to explain she was safe. Instead, though, she'd started running.

Safe was a fairytale.

Irene still wasn't sure when she'd stopped running, but when she had, he was gone and she collapsed behind this building, hiding under cold metal stairs and praying her father would never find her.

Only now though, after a few days of being sober from whatever concoction her father fed her, her mind cleared only to be filled with memories of the dragon.

Her body ached for his touch. Even having only a tease of what the fire of his desire would feel like. Something in her had awakened, pushing through the dead swamp of her soul.

Irene glared at the dancer on stage. She didn't get a happy ending.

She got to smell like sweat and alcohol. She sighed.

Anything to pretend like she hadn't caused harm to more aliens and creatures than she could count.

"A bud," she yelled to the bartender. "And a shot."

He nodded and poured her a shot, her nightly tip. The best part of this job was the perk of being able to drown her own sorrows, as long as she stayed just this side of tipsy. Not a problem when you had more demons in your past than hell itself.

Whenever her past slithered its way back in and the pain threatened to squeeze her battered heart. The liquid fire burned away the pain for a little while.

She yanked at the skirt barely covering her ass.

If it was just dragon-boy in the corner, maybe she wouldn't mind her curves. Unlike her sister, she could eat away her pain. She also just had a body that seemed to like its shape and hung onto it. Her father might have commented one too many times, but at least he'd talked to her.

She let her hand slide away from the skirt. Yeah. She didn't deserve Mr. Purple Eyes. But damn it if her soul didn't ache for him. And why? He either wanted her or he didn't and this skirt would not change things.

"Hey, you bringing my beer?" yelled a guy. He could have just gotten up and grabbed it himself, but then again, that's what Ruby paid her for.

She ran her tongue along her teeth and sauntered over to the guy.

"Sure. Here you go. God forbid you give your liver a few seconds to recoup from your lunch binder. Jackass."

The guy gave her a toothless grin. He was a regular. And not one she liked. Not many of the men were, though.

If only her father could see her now. His smart scientist daughter. The one that had no useful powers except her brain. Yeah, this was the last place he'd ever look.

She shivered, even though the place was warm and muggy. She didn't want to think about her father. Except she couldn't forget. The moment her sister left, he started in on her. He wanted another daughter who was useful, yet controllable.

At least the dragon warriors had solved her problem. Or one of them. Taking her sister. She was safe, thankfully.

Her heart ached still.

Where was Lillyanna though? Would she ever see her again? She'd willingly returned with them. Maybe she should go talk to her own stalker.

She did her job on autopilot. She liked not being responsible for much. She couldn't, anyway. Her mind wandered too much.

Her body seemed to keep going back to the guy in the corner, and she assumed it was because he wanted something from her. Which wasn't okay. Of course it wasn't. Maybe. She hated men. You couldn't trust them. You couldn't trust what they wanted. They were so willing to take.

Then why then did she feel this way? The numb she so desperately clung to fell away as she glanced over her shoulder.

A crippling need filled every open hole in her Swiss cheese soul.

Those eyes. The ones staring into her very being. They were the ones she dreamed about.

He was real.

2

*N*yke licked his lips. He wanted to taste her. The hunger for her had him clenching his hands into fists. He'd watched her for the past few days, the scent of her consuming him.

Mine growled his dragon.

Every time someone looked at her, he'd tried to go to her rescue, only she seemed to not notice. She didn't seem to need him. He needed her though.

Yes. She was theirs. He cursed the goddess as Irene walked around as if she didn't know.

When would he be rewarded with her sweet lips, or fuck he'd settle for a glance in his direction? He fought back his dragon constantly, the pain of his own claws digging into his hand a reminder he was failing.

He'd done as she'd asked, he left her alone. Mostly. Nyke watched her from the shadows. He protected her in her restless sleep and he stood aside every evening.

This was better than the first few days, he supposed. It had nearly broken him to watch her rummage in nearby dumpsters. He should have just taken her, brought her back to the ship, only something told him she would never stay if he did. She wasn't like the others. Something about her edges was rough. Her soul broken. He knew she was his mate, but he could see more than that. Something within her wasn't right, and he couldn't claim her like this.

Here he was. Alone. He hadn't told his brothers he wasn't coming back. Details, details. They had to understand why. Too bad they didn't seem to shy away from his silence. Every time he checked in, it was a barrage of advice.

Deo preached of giving her space. Eadric spoke of patience. Kal spoke of following her lead. Sure, he could do all that. He would give her space, space enough that if anyone tried to hurt her, he'd have little trouble reaching out and killing them.

Tonight was his breaking point. He couldn't take it anymore. His rock solid barriers seemed to wear away as the waves of his emotions surfaced the more he was around her.

Nyke hadn't been prepared to find his mate. Not with someone he'd demonized. A scientist from the compound. Someone that had nearly caused his brother to lose his humanity. Here he was though, fighting back against instinct. Watching her.

He needed to touch her. His dragon grew more and more restless waiting. Nyke struggled to control his need for her.

He would not give in. His eyes followed her barely covered ass as she walked around to the tables. She never came to this side of the room and it pissed him the fuck off. The corner of the already dark room hid him, but he knew she sensed him.

He growled at the burning of his skin as his dragon scratched to be free. Not yet. He wouldn't go to her yet. He didn't trust her, but fuck if his dragon didn't care. They didn't see eye to eye, and that was frustrating. He ground his molars together.

Watching her closely, he tried to see through her. Her eyes always focused anywhere but him. Sharp. Aware of everyone, everyone except him.

He waited. Why didn't she approach him like she did the other men? He'd hidden in the corner every night. She had to have noticed. She needed to come to him. He would not go to her.

Feeling around in his pocket, he grumbled at the empty space. He'd nearly run out of money paying that redheaded woman to leave him alone. He'd have to return to his brothers soon.

"Have you been naughty big guy?"

He glared at the girl.

"No one puts hotties built like you in the corner."

Nyke didn't have a clue what she was going on about. The only bonus was he wasn't invisible, so again why the hell did Irene not come to him?

"Man of few words, that's my kind of man."

He shook his head.

"What's your pleasure? You can't just want to stand here all night?"

Nyke grunted. He could do as he pleased. "I am an elite warrior. What would you do to remove me if what you say is true?"

She giggled, and he went back to looking for Irene.

He froze as a light touch traced his forearm and up the corded muscles to his bicep. He yanked his arm away.

"What's wrong?" He noticed her eyes follow his line of sight. "If you just close your eyes, I can be anyone you want."

Nyke took a step away from her. "I need only one, and you are not her."

She stuck out her lower lip. "All the hot ones have odd fetishes."

He'd look up that word, fetish, later. "Female. I am good. Perhaps you should find better employment for yourself."

He knew he hated his female showing her bits. He couldn't assume this one was any happier.

"I probably make more in an hour than you do in a week," she shot back.

He rolled his eyes. "Female, I am sure you do well. As I am currently on a mission, I highly doubt you can fathom my pay. Please leave me be. I wish you all the best."

She scowled. "Maybe you just need to blow off some frustration?"

She had no idea. "I do," he said.

He jumped as she touched him again. This time though, her hand slid a little too south for his liking. "Careful there, big guy. I don't bite hard."

His eyes bugged. "What? No. Female, please leave me be. You do not bite someone else's mate."

Taking her hands back, she looked at him like he'd just shifted without knowing. He was certain he hadn't. Mostly. His hands traced his own face. Yeah. No issues. Good.

He turned back to his mate. She hadn't even noticed that another female had touched him. Why was this one sided? He'd almost lost it when males touched her. Hell, he'd nearly forgotten himself, he could hardly deal with it.

Nyke couldn't wait any longer for her to come to him. Surely she knew he was there. Could feel his presence. He could pick out the beat of her heart in the crowd and smell her delicious scent wherever she went.

Nyke adjusted his stance and cursed his pants once again as his dick betrayed him. His female taunted him with too small skirts and her nearly out-there breasts. Goddess she needed to cover up. His fucking dick was begging for her while his damn mind threatened to remove her and force her to cover up. No one should see his female. Not like this. Who did she think she was? How could she show off her body to someone else?

His dragon roared in anger at the denial while his brain reasoned them to death. At this point, he wasn't sure of anything anymore. He was losing his steel grip on his own reality.

Once, just once, she'd glanced at his darkened corner and he'd sworn she'd recognized him.

Nyke hated his lack of control. He was the one to plan missions. But right now, the only thing he was in control of was the fact he hadn't ripped her clothes off.

His dragon thrashed around in his soul. He pushed away from the wall, pausing. They fucking hated standing here, waiting for her to see them.

She didn't need to be rescued. What the hell did he do with that?

Fuck no. Shaking his head, he tried to remember that he didn't trust something about her.

A hand gently, but firmly rested on his shoulder, surprising him.

"Female, I said I was not interested."

A breath hissed from his lips as frustration finally boiled over. He was so fucking consumed with her he'd let someone surprise him.

"Yeah, I think we all get that. You obviously see something you like."

Nyke growled as he looked over into the familiar redhead's face.

"She's not one of the dancers, but I have a feeling you know that by now. You aren't going to get far with her, something you also probably know."

Yeah, he fucking got that already. He grunted.

"Look sweetie, you're good looking, you seem smart, I'm not sure what you're doing here. You don't need us. You don't appear to be a man that struggles to find company. Is there more history here than what I seem to be aware of? Ivy has a past and she won't talk, but she hasn't said anything to me about you either."

Damn it. This human needed to walk away. He growled in anger, frustration, warning, Nyke didn't actually know.

"Calm down. I'm not here to dash those tiny little dreams of yours. The name's Ruby, don't forget it. How about you put your time to better use? Like I said, from the looks of things Ivy doesn't have an issue with you at least."

He finally met her eyes and attempted to keep his dragon's irritation down. Ivy? Who was Ivy? He thought back to the last few days, and he'd remember some men calling out the name. He hadn't realized it was Irene they'd referred to. He'd been so busy being agitated that her body was on display and he wasn't allowed to drape his coat over her or better yet his own body. He wondered for a moment why his future mate would change her name. It wasn't for him, so why the hell would it matter?

"I trust her. If she is okay with you, I'm okay," the woman, Ruby continued.

Narrowing his eyes, he spoke. "How do you know she trusts me?"

Ruby laughed. "He speaks. Wonderful." She smirked. "And I know because she hasn't punched you yet."

He smiled. She hadn't punched him. That was a good sign then. And here he'd thought he was getting nowhere.

"Anyway, big guy. I'm in need of a new bouncer. How about you put your big hulking hotness to work instead of paying me to keep this corner company? You keep the girls safe, including Ivy, and you can be here all you want. This place isn't much, but it's all most of them have."

For the first time since coming to this dwelling that had a shitty sign about adults only and two for one well drinks on Wednesdays, he finally looked around and noticed the place was crawling with near naked women.

He could feel his eyes bugging out of his head. How had he not noticed that his Irene had been the only female mostly dressed? He'd been so focused on her; he hadn't seen any other woman. This was not good. What happened if the enemy found him and he was wound so tight he hadn't noticed? Shit.

Maybe having reason to be closer to her was what he needed. Reason to watch her. Reason to keep close.

"Yes."

Ruby smiled as he glanced back at the woman.

"Great. You start now. The rules are simple. You see someone causing me grief, you dispose of them and call the cops if you need to. Work with Trent, the bartender. I pay cash nightly. There are no benefits other than the free show, although you don't come across as someone who seems to care."

He shrugged and found Irene again, watching as she bent over a table and her ass teased him. How the fuck was this his life? He was a sacred warrior, and yet here he was doing a human job. At least he was good at protecting; this job, bouncer, didn't sound bad. He would be able to protect his Irene until he could get past his own head and her walls.

They needed off this shit hole of a planet before that freak of a doctor could find them again.

A scratch of his jawline grated against a five o'clock shadow. It still didn't sit well with him that his brother hadn't found the bastard doctor any more than he enjoyed watching his mate work here.

Finding their mates was becoming more urgent with this new persistent threat. He hated to be without his brothers, but he needed to be here. He needed to gain her trust. He needed to trust her. He needed to see what she knew.

He needed to bury himself deep inside her.

3

*I*rene squeezed her thighs together as a familiar heat settled between them. He was watching her again; she knew it. She could feel the heat of his stare. It was always there. Slowly she turned around, glancing at his corner, trying to hide the fact she saw him. She blinked twice realizing he wasn't there.

A quick scan of the room. Where did he go? Maybe she didn't want to be near him, but maybe she didn't want him not to be.

Irene had battled the static waves thumbing through her body whenever he was near. She fought against every urge to run to him and let those muscular arms hold her. She fought the safety that he brought her and the calm that only he brought. She wouldn't admit it though and give another man power over her.

"Ivy, take that trash out," called Ruby from the front of the club.

The distraction was welcome. She nodded and headed around the bar to grab the black bag.

"Be right back," she said over her shoulder. The bartender, Trent, probably cared. Maybe.

Pushing through the metal door that protested with a squeak into the alley, she stepped into the dry, hot night air.

The sour-sweet of the rotting garbage welcomed her, different from the stale scent of beer and booze. Her skin prickled. Someone was watching her. Irene spun around, but no one was there.

Huh. Maybe she was wrong, except. No. She was never wrong.

"Who's there?"

Nothing.

She took a deep breath, calming her nerves. If it had been her father or one of his demons, she'd already be in trouble. Maybe it was just some homeless person. Or maybe it was someone from the apartments above. She knew people lived there, in fact she had a room in one as well. It was dry and safer than being outside, but that was it for niceties.

Slowly, she turned back to the dumpster. Hefting the bag up over the lip of dented and rusted metal, she released it with a crash and clank of glass.

The heels of her boots click-clacked against the pavement as her pace quickened. Irene rubbed at her forearms. She couldn't shake the feeling, but another glance over her shoulder revealed nothing more. She was still alone.

Reaching for the cold knob of the door she twisted and yanked, quickly sidestepping and yanking it closed behind her.

Logic said the door was unlocked and if someone had wanted to get in they could, but she didn't give a damn about logic. She didn't like the feeling of being watched.

Pulling her hand away, she turned and walked back to the main room, squinting as her eyes adjusted to the lighting.

"Hey, Ivy," said Trent.

She flashed him a smile as she ran her hands up and down her arms, trying to chase off the feel of a thousand tiny bugs running along her arms.

The night of her escape still haunted her, or rather the things she'd left behind but couldn't truly outrun. The nightmares of all the souls she'd seen in and out of the compound. All the cries of every living creature that never left that place.

Except not everything from that night was a nightmare. Even in her haze of fevered pain, her body hot yet she couldn't stop shivering that night. Not until a warm, strong man had lain down next to her in that gross, disgusting alley.

She remembered the pain had stopped, and her mind had cleared. She should have been scared, but he'd given her a peace she craved. Even if he'd been the angel of death, she'd have welcomed the end. His scent, though, had been a giveaway.

Even now, his spicy musk overpowered the scent of cheap booze and she knew who it had been. She'd known that it was her dragon man. He hadn't listened to her. Hadn't left her and deep down she'd been relieved and maybe a little afraid. Not of him, but for him. He needed to stay away from her. She brought death and pain.

"Ivy, table three," Trent hollered over the music, breaking through her memory. She bit her lip still looking for her savior. Where was he? Had he finally had enough and left her? She gasped a wavering breath as a pain hit her square in her chest.

She was well and truly alone. On autopilot, she teetered her way over to the bar, yanking on her top in habit. Well, at least he'd stay out of her father's clutches if he left her. Maybe he could keep himself safe.

A tear threatened to escape her eye, and she wiped it away with the heel of her hand. Not today. She would not grow emotions today. This was her life. A place that housed something raw. A lack of emotion and pure instinct. Animalistic and simple. She could mindlessly hide here.

"Hey, waitress. Where's that drink," shouted the customer. Right. Work. She had to work. Grabbing up the bottle, she turned and headed back to the table. He was her second to least favorite customer tonight. Maybe he'd never been here before. Not a regular. Which was good for business, except he didn't seem to be able to handle his alcohol. Wonderful.

His friends sat around the small booth hooting and hollering as the dancer climbed her way to the top of the pole. Not this guy, though. As she got closer, she realized that her earlier assessment hadn't been right at all. Maybe he acted drunk a few minutes ago, but his eyes were dark and focused on her. Maybe he was a shifter? She hadn't seen eyes like his, not in the lab anyway. The energy rolling off of him chased a shiver up her spine. Yeah, he wasn't a regular, and she'd be happy to never see him again.

"Here," she reached across to slide the beer across the table when his hand darted out before she could pull it back.

Irene tried to pull away, but she couldn't. His hand was an icy stone against her skin. She couldn't free herself. His eyes flashed darker, the blackish-purple overtaking the iris.

What was he?

She had no idea, but something in the recesses of her mind screamed: this was her father's doing. She pulled again, but the guy didn't budge. A spiral of panic laced its way from her stomach to her throat.

Irene tried to shake him off. "Let go of me or you're going to regret it," she said through clenched teeth. Her tone hiding the fear.

Nothing. His dead eyes just stared. "What do you want from me?" she asked. This time her voice faltered.

The man or whatever he was slowly smiled, his lips curving up into what might have looked pleasant on anyone but him.

Her chest tightened. She needed to yell for help. So much for a low profile.

Before she could find her voice, a massive hand planted itself onto the creeps and pulled.

She yanked out her wrist and rubbed where the vice like grip had settled, red marks where his nails had dug into her skin.

"You. Out. Now."

The guy's eyes faded back to dark brown, the black pupil normal. She blinked several times, trying to figure out if she'd imagined it or not. She might have, it's not like her damn mind wasn't on overdrive all the time. A few quick breaths and she forced the air back into her lungs. The rhythm of each breath hitched as the undeniable dance of magic against her skin took over the feeling of fear.

"What? Why?" the guy stammered.

"Get out. You do not touch her."

Irene looked up at the towering beast of a man and lost her breath for an entirely different reason. She hadn't allowed herself to be this close. Not since Irene had nearly jumped from his dragon's back and ran.

Every nerve within her was on fire, begging her to push closer. Begging her to let her guard down. She closed her eyes and inhaled him. Maybe she should.

A shiver of memories from the compound filtered in. Memories she would rather not relive. She'd let the guards use her. She'd always said it was on her terms, but at the end of the day she'd still done things she'd hated. She'd never truly given herself to any of them, but she hated them for using her.

Because of them, the idea of sex made her sick to her stomach. The idea of letting any of them take the one thing she could control pissed her off. This guy, this alien, would do the same. All males wanted was one thing, and she would keep that one thing to herself. She said this, and yet her body didn't agree.

How could she forget those guards? She'd had to gag down her revulsion of touching them to get access to her sister. Sometimes it was access to a prisoner. She'd convinced them sex was dangerous given her father, but that didn't mean they couldn't still use her and humiliate her.

Irene needed to move on. Be in the present. She tried to focus on the conversation, but all she saw was her forbidden rescuer dragging away a guy. She shouldn't want him, or any guy. She nearly fell as one of the guy's friend's knocked into her as they followed behind, yelling and hollering. He wasn't phased and didn't even seem to notice the trail of commotion behind him.

Irene envied his confidence. What would it be like to be free of fear and regret? Hell, what would it be like to not be confused.

"Irene? Are you okay?"

She looked up, meeting the deep purple swirling in his eyes. Her frustrations and fear melted away in those eyes. He quieted her mind.

"Are you okay?" he asked once more.

He also apparently paralyzed her. Somehow amid all this chaos there was nothing and no one but him. What was he asking? Damn it. She was a smart woman. How was she so dumbstruck?

The guy was talking to her. The dragon. Hot dragon who had rescued her twice now. She wondered what kind of name he had. Was it foreign and hard to pronounce, or was it soft and rolled along your tongue like dessert? An image flashed behind her eyes of him kissing her. Her cheeks flooded with heat.

"What's your name?" she blurted?

Oh, that was not what she'd meant to say.

His eyes narrowed. "Nyke. Are you okay?"

Nyke. She liked his name; it seemed to fit him. Huge. He was huge and if she wanted to kiss him he'd have to bend over for her.

A muscle in his cheek twitched before she realized that she'd inched closer to him.

"Are you okay?" he asked again.

Was she? No. No, she wasn't. This man made her forget her past. Her pain seemed to forget it existed with him. What did that even mean?

"I, I think so," Irene backed away from him, not trusting she was going to make any wonderful choices.

Her eyes flicked to the bulge in his pants, and she caught herself licking her lips. Hell no, was all she could think.

She didn't want to think of his bulge in his pants or how it would be to kiss his mouth and taste his tongue. No, she didn't want to think about how his hands would feel running over her curves. She shivered at every thought she wasn't having.

Why couldn't she remember she hated men? She hated the feel of their shriveled little man-bits. Thank God the two guards she'd had to deal with were built like mice. She would never allow a man to use her again. Starting with this guy and ending with her father.

"Why are you over here?" she said, finally finding her voice.

If it weren't for the flash of something in his eyes, she wasn't sure he was even alive. Did he even know how to smile? Not that yelling at him gave him much to smile at.

Irene gave herself a pep talk. She needed to ignore Mr. Way-too-many-muscles. Her eyes flicked to his crotch again. He was definitely not built like a mouse. Gah. What was wrong with her?

Deep breathing. She needed to take more deep breaths.

"Why are you here?" she asked again.

"Protecting you," he growled out.

Her heart swooned while her mind argued and chastised her. No. She didn't need protecting, most of the time.

"Well, I don't need you," she said. She cocked her hip. When in doubt, display attitude, it worked for some animals. She just couldn't remember which ones.

A muscled twitched at his temple.

"That was not what it looked like," he grumbled.

She shrugged. "Well, I can't help it if you think you saw something."

The swirling purple of his eyes seemed to quicken, and the pupil elongated. Irene didn't look away. That was the dragon, she was sure of it.

A moment passed before he spoke again. Why hadn't she

backed away? Something about this man had some kind of invisible power over her. Survival instincts sort of seemed to short out, and she didn't like it.

"I know what I saw, Irene. If you'd prefer, next time some creature grabs you, you can just explain to Ruby why it is I didn't come help you."

Irene jabbed a finger in his rock solid chest, swallowing her desire to run her hands over it. "Don't you tell me to do anything Mr - well, Mr. Creepy-stalker. I see you hiding over in the corner. Like Ruby is going to take a creepy stalker's side over mine. Don't you have something else to do, anyway?"

He didn't move, and her finger was starting to hurt from poking him. Before she could pull the digit away, his hand grabbed her wrist. Tingles of foreign energy wrapped itself around her arm.

"I am not a stalker, sweetheart. I am here to protect your ass. I did not come to this goddess-forsaken planet to let you die at the hands of heathens."

He advanced on her, and she corrected, backing up until her ass hit the wall.

Her breathing grew ragged with every step. She couldn't think of a single thing to say as his lips moved and heat pooled between her legs.

"I grow tired of human games. You know what I am. You know who I am. Don't deny me any longer. I have grown tired of this place." He looked around before capturing her within his gaze. "I grow tired of you flaunting what is mine in front of these pathetic males."

He was a mere inch from her. Her breasts rubbing against his solid chest with each breath. He braced himself, one hand on either side of her head, his face coming closer, his breath warm against her ear as he whispered over the music.

"You are mine, Irene."

Her breath caught. She couldn't think. What was her goal?

Hide. Right. She was trying to hide. What would it be like to hide within this man's arms?

Heat pooled between her thighs and her heart beat double time. For all the things she envisioned in a man, he wasn't any of them. One, good-looking men were rarely smart. Two, her body didn't seem to know she hated all men. It was like he could wake up every nerve ending in her body at a glance. It didn't know her sex drive was dead until now.

No. He wasn't part of getting free. She would be trading the devil she knew for the devil that she couldn't resist.

4

He growled as the scent of her arousal hit him. He pulled in her beautiful scent and his pants grew tighter.

Fuck. This was not how he'd planned to get his mate. He didn't want to take her here, in public, in this pathetic establishment reeking of desperate male.

Nyke hadn't bothered escorting that pathetic male to the door. Or, rather he hadn't needed to as the little male had run away, straight out the door. His friends sidestepped Nyke, confused and staggering behind. This job was much too easy and did nothing for his growing frustration.

He didn't honestly care if they left or not, as long as they didn't touch his mate again.

He sucked in her scent again. Licking his lips, he dared to taste the softness of her neck. The pulse of her heartbeat drew his eyes as he lowered his head. His lips gently grazed the skin. She gasped.

She was not immune to him, as she would have him think.

One more taste. It would tide him over for now. A light brush of his lips and he pulled away.

He needed to back away. Damn it, if his dragon didn't make this harder. She was still the daughter of that shit show of a scientist. How was he supposed to just let that go? How was he supposed to trust she wouldn't endanger him or his brothers and their mates?

The reality was a sober reminder to his soul, and he slowly backed away. Her breasts heaved in air and he barely kept his shit together long enough to put a few more inches between them. His pants chafed. Yeah. Instinct was a bitch.

"No," she said.

He smirked. "No, what?"

"I'm not yours. No."

He laughed. Oh, he was getting to her. "Like it or not, you are mine. When I make my move, you won't be able to say no."

She glared and crossed her arms over her chest.

She was trying to kill him. He could almost see her nipple as her breasts threatened to spill over that damn fabric. Frustration settled in as he leaned into her one last time. "You will beg for my touch soon enough."

Drawing in the air, he moaned at the sweet scent of arousal. The pink of her cheeks giving him a preview of what she would look like on his bed as he made her come.

"Whatever," she said, in between breaths. "You men are all alike. You think all women are yours for the taking. Well, I'll have you know this one is not."

His brow knit and his eyes narrowed. It was one thing for him to have his doubts, but her actually saying no was not okay. Why? Why would she say no when everything about her seemed to say yes?

Fuck if he understood his mate. His anger simmered. Nyke hadn't spent the past few days standing in this damn place, swallowing his pride when men looked at her just for her to tell him no.

No. He didn't want to hear no.

This time she was the one to smirk, and his dick twitched. Why was her attitude a turn on? This whole mate thing was beyond confusing.

"You might say no, but your body says yes. I will be here. Waiting and when you finally say yes, you won't remember why you ever said no, let alone your own name."

Without realizing it, his body was pressed against hers, her soft curves his for the taking.

Her heart thrummed between them. Yes, she wasn't immune, but he still wasn't sure what to do with this knowledge.

Trust her? No. But he wanted her. Maybe just one taste of her mouth. That was all he needed. One taste to keep the dragon at bay. His soul burned for her as he stared into her beautiful, endless green eyes. She wasn't like any female he'd met. Because she was his.

He lowered his head. Yes. Just one taste and then he would back away. Wait, watch, and learn.

Would he regret this choice? He didn't have regrets. He had to be sure all the time. If he screwed up, then shit didn't work.

This would be no different. He wanted this to work. He needed this to work. What if fate didn't actually know what it was doing, though?

His dragon nudged him. He didn't give a shit what Nyke's head had to say.

Licking his lips, he realized just how much he hungered for her. His dragon would no longer be denied. Too many days and nights watching her had worn away at his resolve.

Too many weeks watching his brothers find their mates. Too many nights fighting his dragon.

His eyes danced over her face. She was the most beautiful creature he'd ever seen.

Irene hadn't spoken. Her eyes flashed between green to a darker shade, something he'd never noticed on a human before.

"Beautiful," he said with a breath.

Sliding his head against the soft skin of her neck, he cupped the back of her head. Breathing in her scent, calming the stirring in his soul.

The loud club fell away, leaving nothing but her and him.

He surrendered to the need.

He inched closer, his hand holding her tight while his stomach did a flip. He didn't understand what that feeling was, other than for the first time in his life he wasn't sure of anything.

His lips touched the warmth of hers. Something ran through him at the touch of her mouth to his. Power? Need? Everything he wanted.

Pressing his lips against her mouth, deepening the kiss he wasn't confident she wanted him. He paused. Perhaps this was a mistake. Too much, too soon. He was just about to pull away when she finally answered him.

A sigh of air left her lips as her fingers threaded through his hair and she kissed him back.

Her lips were hungry, and he let her take over. Nyke couldn't have stopped even if he wanted. She could take everything from him she needed and he wouldn't care.

He couldn't control the hunger raging between them. Nyke knew nothing like her kiss. An entire universe of pleasures and joy and he'd never once in his life felt something like this.

His free hand snaked around her waist, pulling her against him as he pressed himself against her, his hard-on teasing her.

Someone cleared their throat behind them and Nyke growled loud enough over the music there was no mistaking his irritation.

Irene pulled away and peered over his shoulder.

"Ruby, I - I'm so sorry. I don't know what came over me."

Ruby chuckled. "I do. I've seen him. Hell, the entire club has noticed him. But, aside from that I hired him for exactly that, his looks. I need him to handle someone who's getting a bit out of hand. Sorry, kid. Intermission."

Ruby's hand rested on his shoulder as she tried to pull him away.

A growl surfaced again as his dragon joined the protest. They'd finally gotten what they wanted and now he was being made to leave and for what? A human job?

Fuck. No. The job was what had gotten him a valid excuse to be near his mate.

His hand grasped air as Irene pulled away. No. She needed to stay near him. He wasn't sure he could fight against the dragon's magic much longer. Deep breaths.

"Go, I'll be around," Irene said, straightening the too short skirt. Her hips swayed as she started to walk away.

He took one step and swore. His pants were too damn tight now. Fuck.

"Come on, Casanova."

He adjusted himself while holding in a snarl. Fuck.

He followed Ruby as his damn heart loathed Irene walking away. They stopped on the other side of the club.

"Go take care of that asshole and you can have Ivy, after hours. Don't you hurt my girl, though."

His eyes narrowed on the prick in the corner. The two young females yelled. He watched as the bag-of-dicks raised a hand.

No. No fucking way would that douche hurt a female on his watch.

Nyke used his superhuman speed, reaching the guy before the guy's hand could even disturb the surrounding air.

"You have earned yourself a one-way ticket to get-the-fuck-out-town," Nyke said, glaring.

The guy's mouth opened and shut as he took in the size of Nyke.

That's right, asshole.

"Fuck, you. This bitch she promised me the best lap dance I'd ever had. Then this one here comes over and tries to get her to go do whatever these whores do and I wasn't done yet."

Nyke bared his teeth. "You do not use those terms for any female. You may leave now or I can show you the door."

The man's lip curled, but he huffed and turned tail.

"I don't need this shit. I can get pussy for free anytime I want."

Nyke didn't pretend to understand what he meant since he assumed the guy was not talking about a cat.

"Right? Like a guy like you could get anything for free. Jerk," said one female.

"You have offended the female for the last time," Nyke said, sick of how slow the male moved. He grabbed the scruff of the guy's shirt and yanked him out the door.

Nyke stood on the sidewalk as the guy swung once, twice, missing and turning in a circle.

"You are unwelcome here, human. Go find a new establishment."

Nothing else was said as the male fished out the keys from his pocket. Nyke could smell the spicy scent of anger on the male, but also fear. Good. Be angry, but be smart enough to know when you've been beat.

Turning around, Nyke realized he quite liked this job. He still didn't need it, but if he had to bide his time waiting for his mate and his brothers' mates for that matter, he might as well enjoy something. He enjoyed removing the human vermin that seemed to find their way into this place.

Perhaps he could fix this place. Make it safe. Taking in the faded paint of the buildings, the bars over windows, and questionable sounds he could hear from blocks away, he decided better of that idea.

He couldn't truly understand Irene's love of this place, but if she liked it he would do what he could. As he walked back in his stomach churned at the scents. Outside didn't smell any fresher, really. His Irene made it all go away. He scanned the room for her.

Fate really made no sense to him. Why would it have paired

him up with the daughter of their new enemy? As if mating wasn't hard enough on this planet. Not one of the warriors seemed to have found a mate the way they'd expected. Females who fell at their feet.

Right. He'd bring that up when they got home. Perhaps there was a translation issue between ancient texts and current day prophecies.

Goddess. Where was his mate?

The stink of the place invaded his nostrils once more as he walked back into the dark and dingy club.

Two soft hands wrapped themselves around his forearm. He looked down into the dark brown eyes of one of the females he's just helped.

"Thanks, big guy. What's your name? Ruby mentioned we were getting a new bouncer. You're much better than the last one."

He grunted. Now, where was his mate?

He scanned the room, ignoring the woman on the stage and the hooting from a few other males. Finally, he found her settled by the bar.

"I'm Kitty Aspen," the girl volunteered.

Nyke tilted his head. Maybe the guy had meant he could get a cat anywhere after all?

"What's your name?" the girl, Kitty asked.

Nyke didn't have time for this girl. He tried to pull his arm away. She ignored his attempt to get away, giggling and gripping his forearm again.

He needed to get back to what he was doing. Or rather, who he was about to do. Goddess, he needed her.

"Not much of a talker, are you?" Kitty asked again.

He tried to pull his arm away, again. He now could say first hand what it must have felt like to be that pole on stage.

"I am glad I could help. I have somewhere to be," he finally said. He glanced down at her and freed himself from her grip.

Quickly he looked back at his target, but she was gone. How? How in three seconds did she disappear? Where had she gone?

A tug on his arm and this was it. He didn't want to be rude to a female, but she made him lose his one desire.

"I told you, I have somewhere to be," he said, as he looked back down in a pair of a familiar green eyes.

"Hey there, big guy. I can let you go," said Irene.

Glancing over her head, he saw the brown-haired female walking away, a forlorn look in her eyes. She gave a finger wave and turned around, heading back to a curtained area.

Irene took his hesitation as disinterest perhaps, but as she released his arm, he stopped her. His hand circling her wrist.

"Never let me go," he growled, fighting the desire rising to the surface. "You never have to let me go."

5

*H*er breath caught at the intensity in his eyes swirling between the dragon she knew was in there and the human she stood before. Her gaze flicked to his hand circling her wrist where a dance of fiery pleasure encircled her every nerve.

His voice, deep and sexy and another crack appeared in the imaginary wall around her heart.

A flash of memory came to her, the night she'd been rescued. That very first night was still a haze. She was free, but the fear of her father finding her meant she wasn't really free. Not yet.

A familiar feeling came back to her. Irene remembered this, the one feeling that made it through the burning haze of pain from the injections her father had administered. She remembered the feel of his powerful dragon protecting her even when she hadn't asked.

She remembered the fear too. The fear that her father would find her and take this feeling of comfort away too. Her truest fear was that the dragon would be how he tracked her down, again.

Breathe, girl. She needed to breathe. Irene didn't want to admit that seeing that woman touching her dragon had sent a shot of rage straight to her soul. She'd watched him like some crazy stalker. She couldn't look away as he scared off one customer. Sure, she could say that she was just like everyone else. Curious about the commotion. But it was the fact she'd glared after one of the girls that nipped at his feet.

Irene didn't want to watch him, but she couldn't stop herself. No, she couldn't not worry about whatever that girl was attempting to do.

It had taken everything in her to not chase after him. It had taken even more control to not walk over and shove that girl out of the way.

Irene hadn't even known his name until a few hours ago. How could she be territorial over a man she didn't even know? Hell, how could she be territorial over a man at all. Only he wasn't a man, or not a human one. He was a dragon, and he made her feel.

Irene hadn't realized a kiss could feel like that. A swirl of emotions twisted and spiraled within her. She didn't know what had come over her but she had kissed him back and she'd be damned if she let some other woman move in even if Irene wasn't sure what she wanted with him.

Her lips still tingled at the memory. Was this how it felt to trust someone? No, that was much too early to say. Even she couldn't deny the pull to him. The energy that danced along her skin as he'd touched her. She'd never felt this way, ever. Not that her father had exactly run a warm and fuzzy lab. Her opportunity to feel anything emotionally had been with her sister and even there she couldn't touch her. She'd only ever touched those that needed her help, but that never brought her peace.

Shaking her head as another dancer took the stage, and the music changed pace, she tried to force out the nightmares. Tried to focus only on him, or at least on the confusion he brought. What had he just said? To never let him go? What did that mean? Was that his choice to make?

"Everyone has to let go at some point." she said, as she freed his arm.

Looking down at the floor she turned back to the bar. Customers. She needed to serve drinks and keep the only job she had right now. The only chance she had of hiding from her father.

A thought passed through her mind. If this guy was here, there was at least one person who knew where she was. And her father was hell bent on finding these aliens. Maybe she needed to protect him, and maybe he could help her.

A quick glance over her shoulder gave her a reason to not only question what she saw but also a wave of relief that he hadn't left yet.

A voice in her head told her she wasn't alone anymore. But that was dumb. So dumb.

Irene nearly tripped over her own feet, forcing her to look where she was going. A smile touched her lips.

"You look like you're happy, Ivy. It's a nice change, really." The bartender loaded a glass with ice. "Is that the new bouncer?" Trent gave a head nod in his direction.

She shrugged. "No. I mean, maybe I am. And maybe he is. He seems to think he is." She wiped the smile from her lips. "Nyke," she said under her breath.

"What was that, Ivy?"

Turning back to Trent, she shrugged. "His name is Nyke." She loaded up her tray.

Trent gave her an odd look. "Like the shoe?"

She wanted to turn around and see what he was doing right now? Absently, she nibbled her lower lip. Was he talking to that stripper again? Was he talking to someone new? Was he watching her? Her heart fluttered, confused and wanting.

"What? What shoe?" She didn't know what Trent was going on about as she hoisted the tray onto her shoulder.

The tray titled, and she quickly corrected her stance. She didn't need to smell like the bar. This was hers. All hers. Her own life. No one here to torture her or treat her like her life didn't matter. Except something was still missing. She shook her head. There was no room for thoughts like that.

Moving her feet, she restarted her body even if she couldn't get her mind to clear. Things seemed fine until that one customer had shown up. The one with the weird black eyes. Still, she'd take this job any day. Anything was better than watching her father try to play God. Or better yet, the devil. He had no regrets over making people suffer. He hardly cared if his own daughters were suffering.

She stood there as the sour taste of her past tried to take over. She'd gotten out, and it was thanks to aliens. Thanks to another creature her father sought to control or destroy. Whatever came first, it seemed.

She was out. And that should be enough. Her lips seemed to tingle to remind her it was enough until he'd kissed her.

She didn't deserve more than this, though. Except, he didn't seem to agree. The tingle of his gaze raced across her skin. He was her guardian dragon. She couldn't understand why, but she knew he was still near. Could feel his energy in the room as if it was something real, touchable.

Irene allowed it to calm the fear and panic threatening to slither its way back into her soul. Or perhaps it fought to escape.

A shiver of panic tried to overpower her. No. It would not escape and her father would not find her. Her feet moved again, and she was able to make her way to a few waiting tables.

"I am strong," she mumbled to herself.

"What was that, sweetheart?"

Irene rolled her eyes. "Affirmations. Something maybe you should try."

He grinned. This guy was a regular. She didn't know what he did for a job, but he always seemed to come at the same time every day.

"Nah. I'm good. I come here for the company, I don't need an affirmation."

Shaking her head, she smiled. "Maybe you could find real company if you didn't come here all the time."

Some of the girls swore by affirmations as they worked towards a goal. Some of the makeup mirrors even had them written in lipstick. She needed to keep repeating it.

"Sweetheart, maybe I come here because I enjoy your company."

A tilt of her head and she fought a smile. "Pretty sure that isn't the case. But thanks for the compliment."

He smiled and sipped at his beer.

"Well, at least here there's no baggage. No drama. No commitment." He winked and turned back to the stage. He didn't hoot and holler. He seemed to just watch. Irene shrugged and walked away. Maybe everyone needed an escape in life.

Taking a deep breath she repeated to herself, "I am strong and pretty damn good at stuffing my feelings deep down inside."

Yeah, maybe she would need to work on things a little. Still she wasn't ready to let go of her emotional vault. The place in her that could swallow everything her brain and heart couldn't handle.

All those victims' souls were buried there. The ones she could help.

Placing a drink down, the next guy barely noticed her and that's how she liked it. She would stay out of the spotlight and she would lock her feelings back up. Only the electric energy tugging at her made her look around for Him.

Irene tried to hide the fact her body was hyperaware of him. He moved and she felt it. Even in her fevered stupor the days before she was found by Ruby, she had somehow felt him there.

Always close, keeping her safe. Why?

A glance over her shoulder caught his looming presence. There he was, holding up a wall near the door. Nyke was her walking fantasy even if she had just now figured out she had a fantasy. Dreams weren't made for the daughter of a devil, were they?

Irene's top suddenly grew too tight as she tried to suck in the air. The laces of the corset top felt more like a prison than the fashion for the strip club.

Licking her lips, she wanted to block out his existence, but she could no more ignore him than she could stop breathing. God knew breathing was harder and harder the more she denied the strange feeling within her.

Fear began to mix with the desperate need to feel him. Maybe she wanted to be loved even if that wasn't right. But, what if loving her ended up getting him hurt?

Lillyana came to mind. Irene had seen her magic first hand, watched it grow more and more out of control and yet the last time she saw her, she looked - happy. Her sister was different in the real world. Even in the pit of the lab, where the feeling of hope went to die, Lillyana had no fears. She looked healthy. She trusted her dragon would save her.

Irene didn't have that kind of confidence. No one was going to save her anymore than they had come to save those poor aliens, Fae, shifters, or any other creatures her father kidnapped.

It was odd that her sister, the one with volatile powers was the one that got saved and was getting a happily ever after.

Shaking her head she had to stop thinking that way. Her sister would have become used and beaten down just like the rest of them. This was better.

A worry hit Irene though, what was her father doing in their absence? If she wasn't there to take the pain away from his victims, they truly would suffer.

Without her, there was no one to release their souls.

She stopped at the bar and put the tray down.

"What's up Ivy?" Trent asked.

She shrugged and readjusted her top. Irene was a master of hiding except from that shifter. Even now, as she feared her father would come for her she still couldn't hide from the dragon. Maybe her father would forget his powerless daughter?

"Nothing, much. Slow night is all."

Trent nodded. "Want another shot?"

She nodded. Maybe that would calm her mind.

He placed two glasses in front of her. "Bottoms up."

Trent grabbed one and she grabbed the other. She enjoyed the feel of the burn of alcohol down her throat. The feeling of free choices.

The world made a little spin for a second as she clung to the bar. Maybe that was the last shot she needed tonight.

"You wanna go out after this? Maybe get some food at the all night diner?" Trent asked.

Irene blinked. "What?"

His lips slid into a shy smile. "I was asking if you wanted to get a bite to eat after the club closes?"

Did she? All she had upstairs were some microwave mac and cheese pouches. "With you?"

His brow lifted. " I mean yeah. That's usually what a date is."

Date? Right. She'd read enough to understand that, but he was asking her?

"Oh, I-"

A deep and familiar sexy voice cut her off. "No."

She whipped around as his hand snaked around her waist.

"You can't answer for me," she scowled. Anger flared in her veins and the itch to punish him. To punish anyone filled her.

She shut her mouth as Nyke's gaze sliced through her.

"I see," said Trent. Only she didn't care what he said right now.

No man could control her. No. This was not okay. Her body nearly shook from pent up frustration.

Irene gripped Nyke's massive forearms and without thinking she let her anger and frustrations flair to life.

A familiar feeling filled her. She could feel his soul, or rather more than just his. His dragon. Their strings of life pulsed in her veins. Her eyes widened as his life thrummed through her, heat filling her.

She shook her head as her breath caught. This wasn't the same. This wasn't like the others. This wasn't like when she released the souls of those tortured by her father.

This thread, his soul's thread, writhed and danced around her magic. Her breath caught as confusion struck. It called to her and she didn't want to let it go. She felt something tugging on her own soul, pulling her to it. A delicious heat of comfort enveloped her.

An audible growl met her ears and something flashed in his eyes. She stopped, releasing him in the blink of an eye.

"Hey, where's my beer?" hollered a customer.

Irene sucked in a breath then another. The ghost of his magic lingered over her body. What had just happened?

"Ivy? Beer. Take it to that guy before he doesn't tip," Trent said, his voice a splash of cold reality.

She shook her head as she walked away. She shouldn't have done that. He hadn't done anything to her, really. Why had he answered for her? He didn't deserve to have his soul shoved out of his body just for answering for her. She needed to get a handle on her damn temper.

A new desire swelled within her. She quickly glanced over her shoulder, was he following? Gripping the beer, she placed it on the table and quickly swung around realizing Nyke was already gone. Where had he gone now? He could move eerily fast.

She needed to catch her breath. Her nerves were tingling with a new need and it was almost too much. She needed a minute to herself. Motioning to Trent, she headed for the back where maybe she could catch a breath.

She reached for the curtain, and a tickle of air on her neck had her rolling her head in it's direction.

The familiar electrical charge of magic shivered down her

shoulder as his words whispered against her ear. "Are you looking for me?"

The magic within her jumped in excitement and she nearly groaned. She liked whatever this energy was. It made her feel different. Alive.

Peeking over her shoulder she smiled. "No. Why would you think that?"

Nyke grunted. "No reason."

Irene tried to play it cool and instead snorted. Right. No. She had zero idea how to be cool. "What if I had been looking for you?"

A gentle heat of his breath tickled her cheek. His chest was pressed against her and she could feel every breath he took, could feel the rumble of his words in his chest as he spoke.

"Then I would say, what can I do for you Dark Angel?"

His words stole her breath, dark angel? What did that mean? She couldn't seem to catch her breath with him this close. Not after feeling him within her soul. She couldn't shake the feel of his soul, dark and yet pure. Strong.

"I'm no angel," was all she said.

His hands gripped her hips, "you saved me."

The air moved as he turned to walk away. Irene didn't think. She turned to catch his arm. He stopped, his eyes traveling from her hand to her chest to her face. She shivered. If his eyes could make her feel like this, what could his hands do?

Her heartbeat pounded in her ears.

"Yes, Irene?"

Shaking her head, she let him go. She didn't have any reason for grabbing him, except. Except what? She was afraid he might disappear and all this would have just been a dream.

She read that book, Alice in Wonderland. At the end of it, it had all been a dream.

6

What had just happened? She'd touched him, and energy had started to pull his own magic. His dragon snarled. She'd connected to his soul, and he'd welcomed it. Only, he wasn't sure that had been her goal.

She was his mate, like it or not. Did she believe it now?

Something within her was definitely dark and unpredictable. He couldn't risk his brothers' safety if she wasn't committed to him. He'd felt the surprise running through her, the want as his magic had welcomed her. What was she?

Nyke hadn't been kidding when he'd said, dark angel. He'd believed that she would be the one to save his soul from being consumed by the power of his dragon. But he knew there was something more too, something much darker.

He needed to get back to his brothers. This couldn't take all year. That strange glimpse into her powers, into her own soul, told him he was getting to her. His dragon pressed against its human prison, growing tired of the game with their mate.

When she came near him, all his doubts and logic disappeared. Damn.

Or maybe he should say all his doubts seemed to change.

He walked away from her, but damn if that hadn't taken more willpower than he'd like to admit. He glared at his devious mate from a distance and questioned his own senses. She had been looking for him; he was sure of it. Fine.

If pride was her game, he would play. He enjoyed a chase. He liked strategy better. He would wait for her. Wear her down. She would find him indispensable soon enough. Only he needed to find her weakness.

Brother, what has Lilly said about her sister?

Nyke waited a moment. He followed Irene's every movement. She wiped down a few tables as the crowd thinned. It was close to closing time, and that suited him just fine. There truly weren't enough people to throw out of the bar to quench his need to punch someone right now. He needed to go back to the ship and train. Only, he couldn't leave her. Not here. This place screamed questionable at best.

Nyke wanted to trust the lady Ruby, but she had hired him for a reason. This planet was strange. Males pay to see women remove their clothing. Back home there was no such thing he was aware of, although he probably didn't spend enough time in the human colonies to know what men did. He would have had no problem getting a woman to remove her clothing for free, though. Not that it mattered if it wasn't Irene.

His dragon only wanted one woman, and right now he would be willing to pay her.

Understanding dawned on him. Desperation. That's what this odd putrid smell was. Desperate men. He was finally under-standing some more human emotion. Damn it though, why this one?

He doubted paying her would help. He was back to square one.

Her curves begged to be his. His hands damn near itched to touch her. At least she wasn't one of the women on stage. No.

Her body was his. He ground his molars as he watched her bend over, giving him an eyeful.

If he didn't know better, he'd swear she was doing this on purpose. That little tease.

She'd be surprised when he finally expected her to pay up what she was offering.

She bent a little further and his dick twitched. He licked his lips. Without concern for where he should or shouldn't be, he nearly flew to where she was and shielded her from prying eyes.

Swallowing, he held himself under control. Fuck. He could bury himself deep within her right now. End his suffering. He sniffed the air and swallowed his desires. He could end her suffering as well, sate her needs. The sweet perfume of her arousal always filled the air when he was near. Her mouth said she wasn't interested but her body said something else.

Why deny what felt right?

Nyke? Lilly said her sister doesn't have a weakness.

He grunted as Irene's ass backed into him.

"Oh," she squeaked.

Her ass pushing against the bulge he couldn't hide, he rested his hands on her waist. Holding her just far enough away that he didn't explode in his own damn pants.

She pulled away. "I didn't realize you were still over here."

Frustration at his brother's words and her lie pissed him off. She knew he was there, he could smell her need for him. Her pupils dilated as she took him in. She knew he was there.

"You say you did not know, but I heard the rhythm of your heart change as I came nearer. I know you lie, my dark angel."

Her lips thinned into a line.

Maybe he should be more concerned, but right now he had no patience for her games.

None? No one has none. He shot back at his brother. He was done asking for help. He would find her weakness.

"Listen here. I don't lie, and if I did, I would have a good reason. Go mind your own business. That's my last customer over there. Maybe you go heckle him to leave once that dancer is off the stage."

Flexing his hands, he struggled against the anger boiling. She had no weakness? That was shit.

And there was a fat chance on this green planet he was going to babysit some fucking customer when his mate was here, ready for him even if she didn't admit it. Maybe he didn't fucking know if she would betray him, because nothing was following the plan, anyway. Perhaps it was time to throw caution out the damn window.

Drawing in a long calming breath through his nose, he backed up. Only, she wasn't his mate yet. He rolled his neck back and forth. He was stronger than this. Maybe. Maybe he wasn't. Goddess help him.

Nyke left her, taking his post at the door to ensure this last male left. He blocked out his brothers, not that they were any help. He needed time to himself.

They, he and his brothers, hadn't known what they were doing when they came to Earth, had they? No. Why did his mate have to be the daughter of the crazy ass scientist hell-bent on capturing Nyke's kind. Someone always needed to hate someone, he supposed, but this seemed to be much bigger than anyone could have guessed.

He needed to claim his mate, but he needed to keep his head in the game. Keep the plan. They couldn't leave this planet with such an evil presence. Perhaps this planet wasn't directly under their protection, but they couldn't leave it to be destroyed.

Humans were one of the few other species compatible with his own. Letting something this evil live would certainly not suit.

Running his hand over his face, he tried to think. His brothers had been trying to research demons. Deo had had the closest call of any of them. He still couldn't figure out the doctor anymore than he could figure out how to defeat a creature with dark magic from another realm. Battling creatures with row after row of teeth was easy. Demons made those battles look like a walk in a park.

Shit, demons didn't fit any mold that they were aware of. How could he plan a mission when the enemy changed within the blink of an eye?

Speaking of, the music stopped, and he looked over at the table where the last male had been. Nyke tilted his head. Odd. Where had he gone?

Scanning the room, he pushed away from the doorjamb as his heart picked up the pace. Where was she?

He sniffed the air and caught a slight whiff of his female. His boots thundered across the floor as he took off towards the back of the club. Her scent grew stronger as he slammed into the rear exit out into an alley.

A scream echoed off the brick and then disappeared. His dragon's sight took over, the darkness no longer an obstacle. They sniffed the air.

Fuck this. He jumped the railing of the three-step metal landing to the concrete and let his dragon emerge.

His beast let out a snort against the burn of decaying food and the stench of evil. They crouched forward, picking up speed as they caught the direction of their mate.

Sniffing the air once more, her scent came to them. A few feet ahead. They were close. The alley narrowed as they turned, darkness filling the space. He could hear her heartbeat. Hear a muffled cry that most humans would have missed. Yes. She was here. His dragon narrowed his eyes, looking for a clue as they stalked the space.

At the end of the alley was a dead end. So where was she and who had taken her?

He moved his head one way and the next, picking the scratch of shoes against the pavement.

There was no challenge in this, but whatever or whoever had

taken his Irene would pay, and he might as well make it as fun as possible.

He breathed in, holding his fire at the ready. After Irene was behind him.

Nyke peeked around a large dumpster, and there was Irene held by a male. No, something else. The eyes were completely black. Wonderful.

His tail swished back and forth in the alley, the cat playing with the mouse.

"Back off, dragon. She is ours."

Nyke looked around and sniffed again. There was no one else there.

"Ours. Master wants her."

Irene stomped her foot down on the creature.

"Let go of me, you creep," she screamed around his hand. His fingers pressed harder against her mouth and his beast sniffed out smoke.

"Master needs her back. Dragon, this is not your concern. Leave us be."

Deo tilted his head. The words weren't human. He understood them, but they were not Nyke from this planet. His translator seemed to know the language. He'd be willing to bet it was something demonic.

Smoke billowed up as he opened his mouth.

Reaching a clawed foreleg, he hooked the laces of the bodice of Irene's top and slowly pulled.

The skin-suite snarled.

"Ours. She is ours. Leave dragon before you regret it."

He snorted. Regret? He had never regretted a thing.

The first thought passing through his mind was that he should spear the enemy straight through the eyes. Every second it was more and more clear that Irene would not be allowed to leave.

Killing that bastard wouldn't exactly help him get to the

bottom of who this creature answered to. Harsh realities. His dragon huffed.

Fine. Nyke pulled his claw away and instead eyed the thing again. Nyke waited for the right moment to strike. He assessed every heartbeat of Irene, every movement of the creature. Weakness, he needed the weakness. The thing seemed to enjoy speaking. Fine.

He shifted back to human form, his dragon less than happy about it. Their hands remained clawed, his skin still scaled.

"Creature, who sent you?"

It hissed. "We don't answer to you, dragon."

It seemed to slowly sway side to side as if it couldn't pick its next move. Irene's eyes were squeezed tight. He needed her to see him; he needed a way to communicate with her, even if he wasn't able to through a mated bond.

"You may not answer to me, but I would like a word with your leader. You see, he is messing with something that is mine."

The creature clicked and chittered for a moment. "Not yours. Ours. He would not like to see his property being claimed by a dirty dragon."

Nyke growled deep in his chest. Not theirs. His. He would die for this female, he would die without her. The way the creature talked, he served someone, but considered himself one of many. Odd. Nyke tried to think of the magics of Earth.

Deo? What magic on earth can control a human shell?

He wasn't waiting for an answer, but if one came to help him figure out what he was fighting, great.

Nyke took a step forward. Little on this planet could withstand his fire. All he needed was the chance to hit the creature and miss his mate.

The creature's head shuttered and tilted, moving in an off inhuman animation. It didn't seem to notice Nyke.

Good. He took another few steps. The creature's head stopped and glared.

"Come no closer, dragon. Master doesn't want to hurt you. Master wants it's child."

Child?

Nyke? Not many. Necromancers, demons, warlock, dark magics.

Nyke didn't need to hear that answer to know exactly what he was dealing with.

Demons. Our dear friend seems to have found his daughter.

Seconds of silence in his head felt like an eternity as he spotted exposed skin along the neck of the skin-suite clad demon.

Fire works against these bastards then? Demons?

He summoned his fire instead of waiting

Most of them, yes. Don't let it in your head.

Nyke didn't need to worry about that. This creature didn't seem to have the ability to or it might have already tried. Nyke kicked something at his feet, a rock or a bit of glass. All he needed it to do was distract the creature, get it to turn its head a few centimeters.

The exact moment the creature moved, he commanded his fire to hit the creature's neck at the exact moment he screamed to Irene. "Duck, now."

Irene ran as he released her. She paused, glancing between the male and Nyke, blinking several times.

Wails of inhuman voices screamed, probably alerting thousands of other demons just like it.

He grabbed Irene's hand as he clutched her to his chest. Turning away from the creature, they were getting away from here.

"Now we run," he said. A sting in his back sucked the air from his lungs. What the fuck?

Quickly glancing over his shoulder, he saw a long tendril extending from the creature on fire. He sneered as the skin melted away, leaving a shadowed black ink like creature. Without hesitation, Nyke grabbed the tentacle and burned the shit out of it, forcing the fire to accelerate and take the damn thing that had the gall to strike him.

Irene pulled him away, and he released the burning appendage and followed. Fuck, that hurt.

Deo, I've been hit. Anything I need to know from a demon attack?

Deo answered almost instantly. *Get somewhere safe and I will come to you.*

His vision blurred as he followed his mate.

"Nyke? Stay with me. I can't drag you up the stairs. Stay with me."

He nodded and followed, fighting the burn seeping through his back. He was sweating, he never perspired. It was a human thing to do. Shit. This wasn't good.

"Where are you going?" he asked. He needed to remain focused.

"My room. It's just up ahead."

Nyke tried to focus behind them. It wasn't chasing them at least. Not that he was certain it couldn't find them.

"Is your place safe?" he asked, his words clipped against the pain bleeding into him.

"Yes. Or well, mostly. I'll explain. Just a few more feet."

His own feet stumbled up the stairs. The pain growing and no longer easy to ignore. Shit. This wasn't right. He shouldn't have been able to be hurt like this.

"Here. Lay here."

On her command, he dropped. A soft surface caught him as he closed his eyes.

This sucked.

7

"Shit. Shit. Shit."

Irene pulled in air against the vice squeezing her chest. What was she supposed to do?

Looking at him, he dwarfed her bed. It surprised her he didn't break the frame as he'd nearly fallen into it.

Shit. She put her hand on his forehead. He was burning up. Then again, he'd just set a demon on fire, so maybe that was normal? Was any of this normal?

"Nyke?"

Irene struggled to keep her eyes on his face, while the rest of him lay there naked. There were muscles on top of muscles and one specific muscle permanently burned into her brain.

She licked her lips and tried to call him again. "Nyke?"

He didn't answer.

Crap. That creature had to be her dad's. Did he know where she was then? Was it the same thing she'd seen in that guy's eyes earlier in the night? Right before Nyke had kissed her? Things had seemed so easy a few hours ago.

What if there were more than one? It wasn't the same human face, so could they hop? Irene was far from an expert on anything her father did. She'd been surviving, making her sole purpose to help those caught escape.

She looked down at her hands again. She'd allowed so many souls to escape the pain or torture of her father. Few ever left the same way they came in. She gasped for air. She could help Nyke if things got too bad, but could she? Could she release his soul? The air seemed thick and she could barely breathe. No. She wasn't thinking this way. He was strong, and he would beat whatever it was her father had done.

"Crap, crap, crap," she mumbled. She wasn't a doctor. She wasn't even really a good scientist. She paced, pausing as he moaned.

"Nyke? Are you okay?"

His eyes blinked open and shut. She reached down and tried to see where he was hurt.

She flinched away as he moved his arm. She couldn't see anything, not with him like this.

Ice. Ice helped fevers. She knew enough to keep people alive; she needed to turn that into a strength right now.

Running down the hall to the small shared kitchen, she grabbed out an ice tray. It wasn't hers, but she'd replace it after.

Baggies. There had to be baggies here. Somewhere. She'd never needed one until now. Drawer after drawer slammed as she tried to find what she needed. Lucky for her, only one other girl lived here for now and she wouldn't be home for a while. She could worry about the mess later.

"Jackpot," she said to herself.

Grabbing out the plastic, she ran back to her room. Pushing against the little rectangles, she popped out one cube easily. Using her nails, she yanked out another and plopped it into the bag. She stepped into her room and slammed into a brick wall.

"Ouch."

A quick glance up and her watering eyes meet Nyke's. Except

they weren't his. Deep purple irises with black elongated pupils froze her in place.

"Nyke? Are you okay?"

He growled, but it made little sense.

"Is that a yes?"

His tongue ran over his lips and his hands jetted out, gripping her hips. The ice knocked out of her hands and skipped across the carpet.

"Crap, that's-"

Her words were cut off as he claimed her lips. His tongue darting into her mouth before she could understand what had just happened.

A moan escaped her at the first taste of him.

What was she doing? He was injured. Right? A hand slipped down to her ass and squeezed, the too short material slipped further up her ass and his fingers found their way under the hem.

Her body woke up the instant he touched her. Heat pooled in her core. This made little sense, but she didn't want it to stop. The magic within her wanted more from earlier. She wanted all of him.

She pushed against him, the heat of his naked body scorching through her clothing. A gasp of surprise followed as he pressed his massive dick against her.

Irene pulled her lips away from his. She glanced down. Holy shit. She'd never imagined a man could be built like that. She wouldn't be able to fit that in her mouth.

Oh, God. What if he wanted more? By the looks of things, he wanted more. She'd never gone that far, she'd never had to. The guards were afraid of her father enough she didn't have to bargain off her virginity.

His irises were still oval, still his dragon.

She raised her hand to his cheek. Fear be damned. She wanted him, wanted to comfort him, wanted to give him whatever he needed.

His eyes flashed between human, and dragon for another second, before the dragon remained. His hand slipped down her hip while the other kept her from moving any further.

Her skirt wasn't serving any purpose at all as he slipped a finger along the seam of her thong, lifting the see-through fabric that was also pointless, especially now.

Her breath shuddered at his touch.

He gently grazed her skin, feathering across her slit before he slid between her folds. Her core contracted at his touch.

"Yes," she breathed out.

Just as he found the sensitive nub between her legs, a pounding on the door had her freezing in fear and Nyke's heading whipping up. She swore smoke escaped his nose.

"Who is it?" she asked Nyke.

He growled low.

Oh shit. What if they were back? No, she was safe here. She'd scribbled the runes she'd seen her father use around her sister's room, around other cells. She knew some were barriers so that demons couldn't track. Some were to seal them in. Others, well, she didn't know what they all meant, but she knew enough to keep her room from being tracked.

Nyke released her, and her body instantly ran cold.

Wait, wait, wait.

"Nyke. No. Don't. Who is it? What if it's one of them?" She tried to keep up with him, but his long strides made it to the door in seconds.

He ripped the door open, the chain popping off.

"Nyke, I have to pay for that," she scolded. She paused, realizing that something huge stood on the other side of the door.

Oh, no. Is this where she died? Or maybe this was her father finally winning. No, she would take her own life before her father could have it back. What she was doing before wasn't living. It was surviving. And it had sucked.

Ice ran through her veins. Her chest squeezed at the fear. What was she going to do? Would Nyke be able to protect her?

Looking up, she gasped at the massive festering line down his back.

Oh, he was definitely hurt.

Without thinking, she raised her hand to the wound, nearly touching it, when the thunderous snarl had her freezing on her spot.

"Down Nyke," the shadow from the dark hall said. He took a step in followed by one other. Her neck ached as she looked up at the three of them. They were all huge, all good looking, and all mostly naked. At least the guests had shorts on.

"Are you related?" she stammered.

The two strangers, one of which she thought looked familiar, looked at her. Whatever. They still scared the shit out of her.

Irene looked over at Nyke realizing markings on his skin were glowing. What was that all about?

"Are you here to help him?"

They weren't attacking, and they knew his name. This had to be a good sign. If it wasn't, she didn't exactly have any other choice.

"Yes," grunted one of them as they lurched forward to grab Nyke.

He snarled and shot back in front of her.

"Shit. He's already delusional."

The other guy, this one lighter in coloring, turned toward her. His orange-red eyes swirled in a beautiful dance.

"You need to hold him so we can sedate him."

She looked between him and the two men.

"How do I know you won't hurt him? And two, or b or whatever, how the hell do you think I can control him."

The one rolled his eyes. "I don't fucking care how. Just do it. If we can't get him sedated, I can't get the poison out of his system. He's in survival mode, his dragon is being driven off of instinct. There is no logic. Now distract his ass."

Okay. Anything to get him to calm down. Right. Okay. Uh. "Nyke?"

He didn't turn to look at her.

"He's not going to listen to shit female. Just do something."

Shit, shit, shit. Okay. She could do this. Something. Right. Something.

She sidestepped around him and turned to face him. Without another thought, she reached on tiptoes and stretched her neck. Thank God the dragon wanted her because he closed the gap and she planted a kiss on him.

It seemed to work because his arms wrapped around her. Internally, she sighed. This felt right, safe, and... Well, and what?

Before she could think, his lips stopped, and he began to fall back. Her eyes flew open.

The darker of the two men stood behind him, catching Nyke before he hit the ground. Thank goodness.

"What are you going to do? Who are you? What did that to him? Is he going to be okay?"

The one brother shook his head. "I'm Eadric. That's Deo. We're his brothers for lack of a better word in English. He will be fine, but we need to act fast. Can you just step aside for a few?"

She gulped a breath of air, and backed up.

"My bed is back there. If that would help."

They both looked at her. "You want to carry his ass?"

The one called Deo shook his head. "Do as the female has asked. Besides, it will be easier for me to remove the toxin if he's not on the damn floor."

One took his arms, and the other took the legs. Both grunted as they lifted him, but it seemed all for show.

She peeked into her tiny room and watched as they laid him

down, rolling him over to expose the wound on his back. It was steaming and began to fester. Odd.

"Is it supposed to do that?"

Deo, the one pulling things out of what she assumed was something like a doctor's bag, answered her. "No. But then again, demon poisons don't follow many rules."

She sighed. She tried to think of what she could do. She'd only ever used her shitty powers to release people from their bodies. Yeah, that was probably called murder in most other places, but when your father was hellbent on destroying the creature, it seemed to be merciful.

Could she do anything else, though? She'd never exactly tried.

"Can I touch him?"

They shrugged. Okay, that had to be a yes.

Irene pressed herself against the wall to make her way around them. Her room was already tiny, but three large men made her room feel like a tiny bathroom stall, only it smelled better, mostly.

Irene flexed her hands. Okay. She could remember what the power felt like when she called on it to push the souls out of their body. Maybe push was the wrong word, but that's how it felt. Maybe she could somehow find the poison and push it out in a similar way. She paused. What if she killed him instead?

The similar fear slammed into her. Her heart squeezed. No. That wasn't an option. She couldn't see a world where he didn't exist. Swallowing, she tried to calm herself and break through the blanket of terror and self doubt.

Laying her hand on his wrist, she closed her eyes and focused. His heart beat called to her, but she ignored it. She ignored the tickle of her power as it sensed what she called the soul. No, that was still the wrong thing. A powerful presence, something dark, pulsed under her fingers.

There, that was it. The presence called to her like the darkness calls to its victims. A promise of power, a promise of your deepest desires. But it wouldn't win, because next to its thrumming beat rested Nyke's strong heartbeat, and she could feel the difference. She could feel the demon's toxic presence.

Using every ounce of energy she had, she pushed against the sick liquid virus. It fought her. Tried to suck her into its dark pleasure and pain. God, pain. How much pain had she known. She didn't deserve the good things in her life.

Irene felt like it could talk to her. Voices surrounded her as she pushed harder. She pictured it being forced into a pool, then a puddle. As she pushed it harder it fought more. It wasn't just a toxic poison; it was still part of the demon itself.

She started to shake against the darkness of it.

It's words of doubt tried to snake their way into her.

She wasn't any better than her father.

She murdered people to feel their power.

She manipulated men to get what she wanted.

A bead of sweat slid down her brow and she tried to focus on its path, it's journey as she tried to ignore the doubt circling itself around her metaphysical self.

"Irene? Are you alright?"

The words seemed worlds away, but they came through her haze. If she stopped focusing now though, she wasn't going to make it. She needed to finish. So close.

It was all rounded up in a pretty little sphere.

She heard someone swear. "What the fuck?"

And then shuffling around.

"Irene. We have it."

She again heard the words, but what if it was a trick of the demon energy? What if she released it and it reinfected Nyke? What if she released it and infected her?

She would never be a prisoner again, and she'd be damned if she allowed Nyke or anyone else to be.

The world tilted and swayed as tiny black dots danced around her vision.

"Irene, it's okay. He'll be okay," came a voice.

She meant to answer, but all she felt was a new calm darkness blanketing her as her arms grew too heavy to hold up.

"Good," was all she said before slumping over in exhaustion.

8

*N*yke woke to the thrumming of familiar music. His head throbbed. Shit.

Brother? Are you awake?

Nyke knew that voice. Fuck. What had happened?

I'm fine. I think?

A shadow moved in the room's corner, Nyke pushed up from the bed, fists clenched as he readied himself for an attack.

"Stand down. It's just me."

Deo approached him, with both hands raised.

Thank the goddess. His head swam. What the hell had happened? "Shit, man. Don't do that."

Deo nodded. "I wasn't trying to scare you. Sit down. Irene had to go to work, and she asked me to come back and check on you. I would have anyway, but it was nice to see the female is coming around."

Nyke snorted. Right. Coming around.

"Right. She left me, didn't she?"

Deo shrugged. "It wasn't without a bit of a fight on my part. She was torn between her duty and your health. I couldn't handle her pacing, so I assured her I would get her the moment you awoke."

Nyke hated the swirling of the room. He needed to get to her and make sure she was safe at the club. He closed his eyes and sniffed the air. "Am I in her room?"

Deo's heavy footsteps stopped. Nyke really didn't care what he was doing. "Yes. I suppose it is the females room. I replaced the lock on her door you busted last night. Do you remember that?"

Nyke rubbed the back of his neck and pushed himself to sit back up. His stomach churned. It didn't matter. He needed to fight through this.

"No. None of it. I remember a fucking demon came after her. No, not just a demon. A minion of her father's."

Deo brought a scanner to his head. He checked the readings and nodded. "What makes you think it's her father?"

Nyke could see the muscles in Deo's jaw clench and flex. He had a bone to pick with the guy, just as much as Eadric and himself. God, that guy had done a number on his daughters. What kind of fucking man would attack his own kids? Nyke couldn't exactly see himself as father of the year, but he knew if the goddess blessed him to have younglings he would protect them the same as he would his mate.

"Is Eadric having any issues with Lilly? Has the bastard found you yet?" Nyke asked.

Deo shook his head as he meticulously checked a vial. "No. We've moved the ship every few days, though. Here, take this."

Nyke took the tube and downed it without a second thought.

His mate. He needed to see her. A flash of her lips against his had him stopping in place, that and the throbbing in his head.

"What exactly happened last night?" he asked.

Deo grabbed something else from his bag and looked at Nyke's back.

"Brother, you had a bit of a run in with that demon. It was

stronger than expected. In dragon form, the demons in that warehouse took longer to get to me. We now know that in human form, shit goes wrong faster."

He flexed his back muscles. It felt off, but nothing hurt.

"Damn brother. You seem to have perfected your treatment," Nyke said. He reached a hand over his shoulder. Rough skin, scars, the only thing that met his touch. Nyke rubbed at his shoulder. It all felt fine.

"That's the thing. It wasn't me. Or, well, most of it wasn't. By the time we got here, you were already too far gone. Your dragon was doing what it could to keep you going. If it weren't for Irene, I'm not sure your recovery would have been this successful or this fast."

Irene? That had his attention. What had she done? He knew he felt power in her every time he was near, but he also assumed that was just how it felt to be near your mate. Fate made it hard to resist your soul's true purpose.

"What did she do?" he finally asked

Nyke eyed his brother putting away something.

"Deo. Do not stall. What did she do?"

He cleared his throat. "I don't actually know. One minute she was by the door, the next she was asking if she could touch you. Far be it for me to keep any of our mates away. I figured it could help you remain grounded during the extraction. She shook and a few minutes later an orb of what I assume was the demon's toxin sat at the surface of the wound. I was able to jar it. Here."

Deo handed Nyke the jar. A small part of him wanted to shy away from the shit as it writhed inside.

"Why is it moving?" he asked

"Your guess is as good as mine. The toxins in my wounds were nothing like this. But again, they were neutralized and removed differently. That and the magic of the dragon had something to do with it. It could be because you were mostly human when infected, or possibly the way it was removed?"

"It's almost like it's still alive?" Nyke added.

"I'm going to take it back to Aisha and see if she can nullify it. Until then, try not to get attacked anymore. You're here to protect your mate until she agrees to come home. For your sake, I hope that's soon."

Nyke went quiet for a moment. He didn't remember any of this, but damn if he wasn't sure he could be more pissed off than when his brothers had been attacked, or their mates threatened. He'd just hit a whole new level of fucking irate.

"This fucker needs to go Deo. We can't leave this planet with his evil still around."

Deo nodded. "You're not wrong. All of us have been in agreement for some time. Lilly keeps asking for her sister as if she might be a key to all of this. She is the only one who has ever seen him in action."

Nyke's head still had a tiny cage match going on with his left lobe and right lobe, and he wasn't sure either side was winning.

"Here, take these. I can feel your discomfort." Deo handed Nyke some pills.

"I will do what I can with Irene. I don't want to push her. Perhaps Lilly was a prisoner, but the way Irene acts, I don't know that she fared much better. Only I can't tell yet. The way she guards herself tells me there is a lot more we don't know about daddy-dearest."

Deo nodded and headed for the door.

"Nyke, be careful. Your female might be your mate, but she knows more than she is letting on. Look around this room. There are too many demonic symbols here for my liking. Watch your back, brother."

Nyke nodded and listened as Deo left. The thrum of music reached him through the floor. Damn, this room sucked. He knew where she lived, he'd spent many nights on that fire escape, but he'd never truly seen inside, not until now. They were directly above the club.

He figured he might as well head downstairs, except he didn't have any clothes. Grabbing her sheet, he wrapped it around himself. Humans and their stupid idea of modesty. Fine.

Stepping out on the fire escape, he climbed to the roof where his bag was stashed.

He pulled out clothing he'd purchased. A black shirt, black pants, black boots.

He climbed back down to the street, his head hurting less and less. Well, at least whatever Deo had given him would work to get him through the night. Goddess, he hoped this night would go better than last night.

Nyke clung to the hope that her wanting to touch him was a good sign. Maybe something changed if she'd allowed him in her room.

He pushed through the front door, his eyes quickly adjusting to the horrible light show from the stage. Where was she? He needed to talk to her now.

Before he got more than five feet in, he was stopped.

"Now, now. I was told you were attacked in the alley while stopping a rape. Do you really think you should come in to work tonight? I called in the other guy, he'll be just fine."

Nyke glared. He wasn't some frail human. He would be just fucking fine.

"I am fine, Ruby. Thank you for the concern."

Ruby frowned. "Stubborn ass men. Ivy told me what happened, and that girl doesn't need more shit. You did me a solid watching out for her. Really, take the night off. I'll even pay you if that's the issue, although seeing how you've been in here every night even before I paid, I doubt that." Ruby sighed. "She's in the back, covering up a bruise from last night. You take care of her. From the looks of things, you're not leaving, are you?" Ruby patted him on the shoulder.

He shook his head, and she stepped aside. Nyke headed

straight for the back. The back. It sounded ominous, but if she was there, he was going.

Nyke pushed past the curtain that acted like a door and paused. There was a hall to the left he hadn't ever noticed. Well shit. He could hear noises that didn't sound like just dancing. How had he missed that before? He sniffed the air, trying to pick out Irene. His nose wrinkled. Definitely not just dancing.

He picked out her scent and followed it in the opposite direction. Pushing the door ajar, he scanned the room where several topless and some robed women were. In the corner he saw the back of his Irene. Someone stood in front of her, dabbing at something.

"Irene? Are you okay?"

She spun around and nearly knocked over a table full of tubes and small colorful pallets.

"Nyke? You're awake?"

She ran up to him, jumping into his arms.

"Damn, wish he'd saved me," said the one who had been dabbing at Irene.

"Ivy, introduce us to your man snack?"

Another woman smiled. "Something tells me our new bouncer isn't just a bouncer, hey Ivy?" The woman winked at Nyke and he wasn't sure why.

Irene released his neck and he put her feet back onto solid ground.

"Lola, this is Nyke. Nyke, Lola." A few more females came over and Nyke tried to shy away. The only female he wanted was standing in front of him. He took several steps back until his back hit the wall. His eyes grew wider and wider.

"Nyke, these are some of the dancers. They were helping me cover up this bruise."

She slid her hand into his, and his heart steadied. How was she okay with all these women near him? He'd have already beat off any man within a few feet of her, let alone fawning over her.

"Ladies, if you don't go finish, you'll miss your cues. Go." Irene's eyes darkened as he watched her features. Ah. Never mind. She was just better at hiding her displeasure.

He pulled her into him. "Are you alright, mate?"

She pushed away, but at the last second she placed her cheek against his chest.

"I am now that you are."

Letting her go, he gently pushed her out a bit and lifted her chin.

"These marks? They are from the demon?"

"Shh." She gave him an odd look and then spoke ridiculously loud. "Yes. They are from the guy who attacked me."

He mirrored her odd nodding until he realized. Right. Correct. Humans. They didn't always know everything about the supernatural world. Although around here he found that hard to believe.

"Yes. Of course. Do they hurt?"

She shrugged. "No more than I'd expect. How is your back?" she asked, her voice back to normal.

He stood up straight, making a show of flexing his muscles and stretching. "Never better."

He took her hand and pulled her back while he lowered his mouth to her ear. "Thank you."

He couldn't help but notice her body stiffen.

"For what?"

He didn't like that she would hide who she was or what she could do.

His lips touched her ear. "For saving me."

Her breath caught. "I didn't. It was your brother."

Pulling back, he looked straight into her eyes. "You are a horrible liar. But I will trust you. If you have a reason to hide this from me, I will give you your time."

A half-hearted smile touched her lips.

"Ivy, get back over here and let me finish covering up that asshole's handy work."

She reached up and gave him a peck on the cheek. "Come find me when the club closes."

Find her after? Who said he was ever losing sight of her again. Backing up he leaned on the door frame.

The female painting his mate's face with some odd-looking cream kept looking up and whispering. It would have been easy to try to listen in, but Nyke was honorable. He wouldn't eavesdrop. Maybe. For now. Or maybe it was that he was still too damn confused about the kiss on the cheek. What had happened last night?

Something about her seemed different. And she wasn't frightened. He studied her, studied the flick of her gaze back to him before getting yelled at to turn around. It was like she had confidence?

"All done. If we need to reapply one more time tonight, let me know. Don't spill on yourself, again," said the female. What was her name? Irene had just told him. Lola? Sure, Lola. Not that he'd ever need that information again.

Waiting for Irene to pass him, he followed her out.

After last night he wasn't looking away from her once, not that the too short skirt hurt at all.

9

a smile crossed her lips as she walked back to the floor. A power she'd never known surged through her. Maybe it was knowing he wanted her as she sauntered away, or maybe it was knowing what it felt like to save someone. Save him.

A weight seemed to have lifted last night, after Nyke wasn't dying, anyway.

She reached for the curtain to step back into the human world. She paused as his hand covered hers.

"Allow me."

She nodded. Irene had no clue what any of this was, but she liked it. Liked the idea that someone wanted to protect her. Liked the idea he had taken on one of her father's minions. She loved the idea that even sick and wounded, he wanted her.

"I like when you smile," he said, the back of their hands gently brushing as they walked side by side.

Heat chased up her neck.

"What, might I ask, has you smiling?" he asked.

She shrugged. There were so many things to smile about. Where could she even start? The memory of his hands all over her? The fact she'd saved him, and okay, that didn't atone for everything, but it was a start. Maybe the biggest of everything was the fact that she trusted him with her soul. Yeah. No. She would not start there just yet.

"Just glad you're okay."

She snuck a glance up at him. His eyebrow cocked, and she couldn't help but take in his perfect chiseled features. He was much too beautiful to want her, and somehow he did.

"Hm. Okay. Yes. I am also glad you are okay too," he responded.

She turned away, heading to the bar but stopped as his hand gripped hers pulling her back into him.

"Do not leave my sight tonight," he said and planted a kiss on her.

As he pulled away she collected herself, but damn if she didn't see stars.

The memory of what else this man promised set a fire burning through her. How many more hours until this place closed again?

Nibbling her lip, she walked to the bar and grabbed a loaded tray. She was officially on her own little planet right now. Who cared who ordered what.

"Ivy? Table three." Trent tapped the counter. "Glad to see you smiling again. He's a lucky guy."

Irene blushed. "It's nice to smile again," she said.

"Oh, and don't tell that guy, but he has my respect for protecting you. Any man willing to put his own life at risk has got my blessing to date you." Trent winked and went back to cleaning glasses.

Irene didn't actually care who approved, but maybe it meant something that someone else cared about her happiness? It was strange. No one had cared about her a week ago, and today she had a small bedroom rent free until she could afford more, a few girls who had come to her aid to hide the bruises, a bartender who watched out for her, and a dragon who bordered on stalker but she liked it.

How had Lilly gone from being expendable and hated to looked after?

Irene's chin seemed to sit a little higher as she walked between tables. The night flew by as she imagined a future. Silly movies that she'd snuck to her sister came to mind, ones where the girl got the guy. Others where the guy proved his worth to the girl. So simple in concept unless you never had the guy. Maybe now though, she did.

A tingle ran the length of her spine. Peeking over her shoulder, Nyke stood at the door watching her with dragon eyes as she wiped down the table.

Maybe she bent over a little further than necessary right then and there, giving him an eyeful. Heat pooled between her legs as she remembered the way he'd touched her last night. She stifled a moan.

The silence of the place and the lights coming on for cleaning barely registered. Irene was in her own little fantasy.

"I believe the table is clean," said Nyke's voice from behind her.

She swallowed. Her ass pressed against something hard as she stood up.

"Is it? Clean?" she teased.

His fiery breath whispered across her ear. "Yes. And everyone has left. We're the last ones. Ruby said I could lock up once you were done."

She dropped her rag, while her other hand slid down his side, moving between them, down to his massive bulge.

"I'm done," she said.

With lightning speed, he turned her around, her head cradled in his palm.

"No, we haven't even started," he said as his lips claimed hers.

Irene ran her hands through his hair as his hand grabbed her ass. Seconds passed before his other hand grabbed her other ass cheek and lifted her. She wrapped her legs around him, pressing her core against him.

She wanted more. Needed more pressure. She needed him to touch her, everywhere.

His kisses grew fevered. "I need you, now," he said between nibbling at her swollen lips.

"Yes," she breathed out.

"You are mine," he said.

Her body burned hotter at the words.

"Yours. Yes." If he kept kissing her neck like that, he could have whatever he wanted.

"Mine," he growled as his hand slid up her thigh.

Her core clenched in anticipation as the backs of his fingers slid over her skin, pushing aside her panties. His touch feathered along her slit, before he parted her, slicking his fingers in her juices.

"More," she begged.

He slid a finger in, abrupt but welcome. His thumb pressing against her sensitive clit, while his finger stroked her on the inside.

She was lost in sensation as a new burn began where his finger stroked and continued up into her belly. She couldn't get a deep breath.

"Oh God," she moaned.

"Mine," he said.

As he growled out that last word she exploded around him, her body quaxking around his fingers.

A few seconds passed before he removed his hand and her body shuddered again. She was burning up and yet the room was cold without him. She wanted all of him. Not just a piece.

"More. I need more," she heaved out between breaths.

Her head lolled back at the sight of him licking his lips. She liked where this might be going, but she didn't want to wait any longer.

"I want all of you," she whispered, looking up and staring straight into the crazy purple-blue swirling eyes.

"All of me?" he asked, as he walked with her still wrapped around his waist.

"Yes, all of you." She didn't look away, didn't blink. She needed him to understand.

"Do you understand what I offer you?" he asked, his brow furrowed. His eyes were intense.

Nyke stopped, pressing her against a wall with his body. Irene couldn't help it, but as she spoke she rubbed her wetness against him, pressing against his obvious hard-on.

"No, but you can explain it to me later. Whatever it is, I am yours."

His eyes darted across her face before capturing her gaze once more.

"I offer my soul to you. Forever." He leaned in closer. "Are you ready for forever?"

Her brain tried to scream no, but her heart overrode it. There was no logic to the safety she felt with him. There was no logic in how years of fear and pain melted away with this man with pretty eyes. No, logic didn't have a place when her heart, no her soul, knew that what he offered is what she'd missed her entire life. He was made for her.

"Yes, forever."

He claimed her lips, hungry. Pressing his dick against her, she reached between them and unbuttoned his fly. He sprang free and her hand wrapped around him. Her body nearly came in response to the smooth hardness as she stroked him.

She'd never imagined wanting to touch a man. Never imagined finding it a turn on. But here she was, desperate to please him. She liked the way his chest rumbled in pleasure as she moved up and down the shaft.

His kisses left her lips, making a path down her chin to her neck. She let out a shuddered breath as his hand grasped her breast under the thin top she'd worn tonight. Nothing but cheap lace to hinder his touch. She'd never felt so sexy in her entire life.

"Nyke, more." She moved her own fingers between her legs, coating her hand in her own slickness. She wanted him. Needed him to erase her past and give her a future.

He raised her up as she held her panties aside, feeling the heat of his erection against her entrance. His eyes watched her as he slowly let her down on top of him. Slowly sheathing himself inside her. Slowly lifting her and reseating her. Stretching her. A painful, yet delicious burn of her virgin muscles taking him in inch by inch.

His eyes never broke from hers. She held her breath as he pressed in further this time, deeper, and a strange stinging greeted her. He paused.

"You are alright?"

Breathing again, she nodded. Because yes, alright couldn't even summarize this. She felt alive.

"Yes. More."

He did as she asked, and suddenly she felt the weight of him deep within her. He kissed her again, pausing a moment while she got used to the feel of him. Slowly he moved, retreating and pushing in again. Over and over, each time a little faster. Rougher. Desperate.

She invited the rough assault on her senses. The reminder she was alive. Free.

"More," she begged.

He answered by slamming into her. She gasped in surprise. Her eyes nearly rolling into the back of her head. A few more strokes like that and she would come again.

As if he could read her mind, he started this new rough pace. The surrounding air seemed to buzz, everything around them disappeared. All she could feel was the heat of her body, the pleasure building with each new thrust.

Yes. More. She would take everything he had.

He thrust once, twice, three times and her muscles clenched around him, taking from him, begging for him to join her. She nearly forgot how to draw her next breath, and damn, she didn't care.

Before she could remember her own name, he slammed into her and roared as his head sank to her shoulder. Irene's world exploded around him again before she'd even been able to recover from the last orgasm.

Her shoulder burned, her muscles quaked, and her magic tingled with electricity. She was liquid and the only thing holding her up was her big, sexy, and protective dragon.

She slipped against his chest as he raised his head, gently licking the spot on her shoulder that tingled. Her breath hitched at the new sensation.

The strange motion sent a whole new wave of pleasure through her and without reason she came again, this time she couldn't hold in a scream of pleasure. Every time she came was stronger, and she was sure that she wouldn't survive. Only she did, every time. .

He gently kissed her as she came back down from her own personal heaven.

"Are you alright, my mate?"

Irene couldn't come up with words, she nodded as he rested his forehead against her.

He chuckled, and if she would have been able to, she probably would have smacked his smug response. As it was, she wasn't even sure she'd walk again.

"I am going to put you down, my dark angel. But only for a moment to fix myself. I will take you up to bed."

She slumped against the wall, trying with little success to push her skirt back into place and cover herself. A smile formed on her swollen lips as his hands brushed her thighs. The backs of his fingers brushed her sensitive skin as he finished the job for her.

"You did that on purpose," she said, her voice breathy.

"I would never." A smirk tugging at his lips.

He lifted her, one arm under her knees and the other around her back. Wrapping her arms around his neck, she let him take her as her head leaned against his shoulder and her eyes suddenly became too heavy to stay open.

"Rest, Irene. You're going to need all your energy for what I have planned," were the last words she heard before he carried her off into her new life. Or at least her bedroom.

1 0

*I*rene's beautiful ass pressed against him as he stirred. Nyke grew hard at the memory of her body, so tight and wet for him. He had allowed her to sleep for most of the night.

He couldn't get enough of her beautiful full breasts, or the way her breath came in little stuttering breaths as she grew closer and closer to coming for him. He was learning her body, every whimper, every quiver.

He wanted to learn every cry, every moan, every inch of her. And now was a good time to start. His fingers brushed the mark on her shoulder as they moved down to claim her breast. His thumb and forefinger pinching at her nipple, watching it harden as he played.

A small moan escaped her lips as she arched her back, her body pressing into him. His hand fluttered down her ribcage to her stomach. Her breathing hitched as his finger slid over her clit, down her slit, over her core. She lifted her leg for him as he teased her, dipping just the tip of his finger into her tight muscle.

"More," she breathed out.

He dipped his finger in deeper, pulling it out quickly, careful not to give her too much just yet. He liked the sound of her heart beating quicker as her need built.

She was already wet for him.

Taking a second finger, he feathered the digits over her entrance, teasing the well-used muscle. She lifted her hips, and he met her need. His fingers slid in, stroking her on the inside.

He needed more.

Rolling over, he positioned himself over her. Pushing her legs apart to make room for him.

Her breathing already ragged, her breasts rising and falling with each inhale and exhale.

He licked his way down the curve of her stomach to his favorite V between her legs. He barely flicked her bud with his tongue and she nearly jumped.

"Are you alright, my mate?" he asked, his tongue poised, ready to lick again.

"Yes, just sore," she breathed out.

He smiled. He knew he hadn't been gentle, the first or second time. He couldn't help it, and she had asked for it. Begged for it.

"Shall I stop?"

Her head rose in a flash. "What? No."

He chuckled. His dragon had been starved of his mate for the past week, or for a lifetime. He wouldn't have been able to stop without some extreme self-control he wasn't sure he possessed right now.

His need for her had been growing and growing as he'd watched her strut herself for all those men. Or maybe it had all been for him. He didn't care now, because she was his.

His tongue lapped at her core, gentle. Her fingers running through his hair told him all he needed to know. He would make this one last much longer. Much slower. She would take from him what she needed this time.

The scent of her beautiful aroma of need floated to him with each lick. She responded to his touch, just as a mate should. He loved the power. He also wanted her to know she had the same power.

Kissing over the same path he'd licked down her, he rose above her.

"Mate, good afternoon. Are you happy?"

She moaned and stretched, pushing her breasts up against him.

"Mm. Yes. My view in this place just got much better."

He smirked.

"Should we eat? Assuming you are not yet ready to leave this establishment, they will expect us to work in a few hours."

This time it was her turn to smirk. Nyke wasn't sure how to take this until she pushed him back and pulled herself up.

"Lay back and I'll show you what I'm hungry for."

His eyes grew wide. Nyke didn't fully understand her meaning, but he could guess and he was growing to enjoy Earth much more.

"As you wish," he said.

As he lay back, she crawled up his body. Her breasts swayed with every movement. Her eyes brightened with desire and her scent grew stronger.

As she came to his dick, she flicked the already erect tip with her tongue and his head lolled back onto the bed. She swirled her tongue around his shaft and he was certain she wouldn't be able to fit all of him in her mouth and he didn't fucking care. His eyes nearly bugged out as her beautiful lips stretched around him. Her tongue wiggled, and she pulled her mouth up and then back down.

She stopped, her eyes meeting his as she licked her lips. His dick twitched with anticipation at whatever his dark angel had in store for him.

What was she doing to him?

Nothing was more beautiful than his flushed mate moving to position herself above him. The heat of her beautiful core above him, already slick and wet, gently pushed down onto him. Her breath hitched as she slowly, painfully slowly, seated herself onto him.

He would let her do what she needed, but damn it, it might kill him.

* * *

He kissed his mark on her shoulder, watching the mirror as his own tattoos spiraled along her shoulder with each touch.

She shivered. "I guess I shouldn't wear a tank top tonight."

They stood in the bathroom as she wiped away the fog on the mirror.

Lifting his head, he crocked a brow. "What is a tank top?"

She flashed him a smile. "The shirt with the little straps. I don't need everyone to know that I'm one of those crazy girls that gets her boyfriend's name tattooed on their ass."

Nyke looked down, and she slapped at him. "Not literally. I mean this." She pointed to the spiralling marks. "This is pretty much the same thing."

He enjoyed the peek at her ass, but understood what she meant. "Yes, same thing. Although boyfriend? I know what this word means, and it is wrong. Mate. You are mine forever."

Turning her around, he pressed her ass against the sink as he bent down and claimed her lips. He needed to taste her.

Brother, is she coming back?

Nyke sighed and pulled away from her. They were supposed to be getting ready to go to the club.

Not yet. Soon, brother. Soon.

He ran his hand over the side of her face, pushing aside a damp strand of hair.

"Would you come home with me?" he asked.

Her face fell. "Home?"

He nodded. His fingers ran alongside the soft skin of her neck, to her shoulder, to her breast.

"Like forever? With you?"

Nyke paused. "Yes. Forever. With me. We will go back to my planet soon enough. For now, you will be with me, here on this planet on our ship."

She gripped his wrist. "My sister?"

Nyke nodded. "Of course. All the females."

He didn't know how to read her. The air was calm, her scent nothing different than it had been moments before. Not fear. Not happy or aroused.

"She's safe then. Really, truly safe?"

He cocked his head and brought her hand to his lips.

"Yes, my dark angel. She is safe and awaits for you to come home."

Irene's lips slowly spread into a smile. "She's waiting? For me?"

Where was this going?

"Yes. Of course. You are her sister. She's been worried. Lilly went back for you at the lab. Or well, one reason she went back."

"Lilly?" she repeated.

"Yes, Lilly. Your sister?"

This time something strange happened, and he didn't know what to think of it. A tear ran down her cheek.

"Are you hurt?" he asked.

Shaking her head, she sniffled. "No. Happy. She doesn't hate me for everything?"

Strange these women were. Tears when she was happy? He'd never understand. "No. She speaks highly of you. She's been begging Eadric to find you ever since the lab incident. I wasn't sure you were ready to come to the ship yet, and Eadric won't allow her out yet."

Irene laughed. "Someone can control my sister? Well and truly control her and she's okay with it?"

Nyke smirked. "I think okay with it is subjective. She gives Eadric enough hell. But, yes. I would say overall she's satisfied with her mate."

Pride filled Nyke as Irene's eyes raked over him.

"If she's a fraction as happy as I am, I would imagine she would be okay with it. Are you all this devoted?"

"We all would die for our mates. Your pleasure is our pleasure. Your pain is our pain. Yes, we are all this devoted as you put it," he said, placing a kiss on the tip of her nose. "So mate, what is your decision?"

She huffed a sigh. "I don't think I have a choice, do I?"

Nyke processed this idea of choice. By definition she could say the word no, but by the goddess he wouldn't accept that answer ever. Somehow that seemed like the wrong response.

"You have always had a choice, my dark angel."

She pursed her lips. "Am I supposed to like that you call me dark angel?"

He touched her temple and decided now might be the best time to see if she was fully connected to him yet.

Can you hear me, here?

Her eyes grew round and widened at his every word. To her credit, she moved her head up and down.

Good. Now, to answer your question, see what I see.

He gave her the visions of her, the first time she'd touched him and then when she'd saved him from the demon poison. He let her feel the darkness she posed as well as the beauty and love that he felt with her magic around him and in him. His dark angel with so much hurt and sadness around her brought him hope, love, and light.

He pushed a strand of hair behind her ear. "You are the only female I could imagine fighting such evil for me. You're my angel, but you're also not innocent. You hide too much pain. It's your curse, but in your pain you have saved me."

She didn't speak for a while, and he had to wonder if he'd said the wrong thing. The truth. He saw her. He saw her pain. Perhaps she thought she hid it well, but he knew she suffered and now, now that he could feel her within him, he could feel her suffering.

Do you feel my power here?

He shifted and held her hand to her chest before bringing her other free hand to his own. With each beat of his heart, hers beat the same. Her magic wasn't of this world, he felt it. Nyke wondered how each one of their mates felt once bonded. How the magic worked between them. He wondered if Eadric felt Lilly's constant flame or if Maddie's magic teased poor Kal. Even Aisha's abilities, did they swim around in Deo's head constantly?

Irene's magic danced along his own as if it were running with his rather than mixing and becoming one. The magic seemed to coexist with the same threads, but never fully combine.

"Yes, I feel you. So that means you can see me too? All of me?"

A peek in her head and he regretted his choice. She winced.

"I can feel you. But, please don't. Not yet. You don't need to see who I was. Who I had to be."

Kissing the top of her head, Nyke pulled her into him. Two seconds in her mind and he could hear the echo of screams. He didn't need to see further to know. He could feel her suffering, and that glimpse at the soundtrack that must plague her was enough to understand.

"I will never see you as anything less, mate. But I will remain here until you either share or learn to block me," he said.

She flashed him a smile, but a tear slid down her cheek. This time he knew it was not joy that filled her.

Nyke lowered his head to hers, kissing along the trail the tears left. He stopped at her lips, hesitating, waiting for her to show him what she wanted.

She lifted her lips to his and pressed her mouth to his.

At first her kiss was slow, but something within her seemed to unwind as he moved his mouth against hers. She broke the kiss and met his eyes.

"I need you to make me forget," she said, and pressed her lips to his again. Her kiss grew deeper, her hands dug into his shoulders. His body instantly took over.

Lifting her ass, he balanced her on the vanity. He ran his hands along her thighs. Her skin pebbled against his touch.

He deepened the kiss, wanting to remove every sad memory in her life. Positioning his dick at her entrance, he slowly pushed into her.

He would make her forget her past by consuming her with her future.

*I*t was somewhere before dawn, and Irene snuggled in his claws. They'd finished the night at the club and then in true over masculine fashion Nyke had cornered her.

Not that she minded being cornered. Her body practically purred when he touched her. All night she had to fight back the growing need for him. Irene had found every excuse to touch him, smell him, smile at him.

You wouldn't have known she had just had sex right before starting her shift, or hell, four times before the day had even faded into night.

She knew she should be content. Holy crap, did she know? How her vagina could feel sore and used and still ache for him the second he came near, she didn't know.

How she could still drool for him across the club. She had it bad.

Irene had heard some of the women talk. She'd never engaged in conversations, just hung in the corner. But she'd heard them. She knew that most women were lucky to come once. It was pretty much unheard of if a man could go twice in one night.

Well, she supposed this was karma. She'd been dealt a shitty hand at life, and now karma was making up for it with Nyke.

Somewhere between being tired and happy, the tendrils of her fear popped up. What if her sister really didn't want to see her? What if her happiness was temporary? What if he said the wrong thing and her bubble popped?

She clung to the massive claw holding her.

You're alright, my mate?

Irene didn't even jump this time, as she slowly got used to him being in her head.

Fine. Just thinking, she answered.

The dragon snorted as they continued to glide through the early morning skies.

Nyke had refused to sleep one more night in her bed. Or rather, he'd called it a primitive torture device.

Part of her assumed this was his way of getting her wherever he considered home.

What are you thinking, mate?

She nibbled her lower lip. *Can't you tell already?*

The dragon's chest rumbled in what she assumed was laughter.

You do not want me invading your privacy. So tell me, mate. What are you thinking?

Irene wondered how she ever thought that giving herself to this dragon would be like selling her soul to something? Something else crept in and she wondered if she'd truly given herself to her dragon because of love, or was it just some other game? No. She couldn't second guess herself. Then again, Irene wasn't entirely sure she deserved this happiness.

What would happen if Nyke saw right through her? Saw the signs of her past? She didn't deserve happiness.

Mate, what are you thinking?

She held onto his claw, realizing just how sharp it was. He was an excellent protector.

I keep wondering if maybe this is all a dream and if it's not, am I being selfish?

They flew in peace for another moment before he answered.

Selfish? What do you mean?

His claw held her tightly, maybe like a hug. Subconsciously, he always seemed to know what she needed.

Selfish that I left my father to torture so many innocent lives while I'm here, happy.

The dragon snorted.

This is the question every warrior asks themselves. Did they save enough? Why were they spared over another? There are never answers. Only the goddess's will.

Irene knew what he was saying. She knew that there was no real reasoning why she deserved to be happy and why those her father kidnapped were dealt their own horrible fate. It didn't stop the horrible guilt. It didn't stop the ache. Just because some goddess had smiled and said, hey Irene, you get to be happy. It didn't erase the countless lives she'd helped free, the countless lives she couldn't.

Nyke? Do you ever wonder if you made the wrong choice? You know, in battle?

The wind ripped around her, her hair tangling around her head. If it weren't for her dragon, she'd be freezing right now. It only took her one glance of her looking down before she realized she didn't need to know how far up they were exactly.

I don't know that one ever knows they were right, not when it comes to lives. I think we all have to trust on instinct to guide us. Trust you have done your best?

Was that true? Did she act on instinct? She was when it came to her sister. She would do anything to make sure her sister was safe. Irene always figured it was best for one of them to be on the outside, and although Lillyanna had seemed like the most dangerous choice, getting her out of her father's clutches was best.

Yes. She had done what she could. She'd let whatever her magic was guide her. She wouldn't have ever known that she was capable of helping those poor souls. Could she have taken care of her father already, though?

Her stomach clenched. Why hadn't she realized that she could have stopped all of this had she just forced her father's soul out? Only did he have a soul?

Mate, I might not be reading your mind, but I can still feel your emotions.

She swallowed. Of course he could.

I worry about all the creatures my father might still have at the lab. Absently she realized she was holding onto his claw so tightly her knuckles glared white.

I worry that if I don't go back, he will take out his anger on them and there is no one there to help them.

Nyke still didn't say anything, and she didn't know if he was good at listening or if he wasn't sure what to say?

It was nice. Nice to finally speak freely. It was nice to be heard.

Trying to push her anxiety away, she searched for her secret box locked deep within her. She waited to feel the weight of it sitting there within her soul where she tried to lock up everything bad. Taking a deep breath, she realized at this moment the weight of it didn't seem as heavy.

A warmth filled her where cold had always lived. Why hadn't she noticed this before?

Our connection can take time, mate.

Shaking her head, she smiled to herself. *I thought you weren't listening?*

The dragon's head dipped. *It's hard when my mate is practically screaming her thoughts.*

Had she been screaming? Right well. She'd been right about one thing. She wasn't alone anymore. Only at this exact moment she questioned if that was good or bad.

It's good, I promise you.

She rolled her eyes. Right.

Irene's stomach blipped, like it did when she used the elevator in the lab. Building up the courage to look out, she saw the ground growing closer and closer. The sky hinted at morning, but they still had plenty of time to sleep. She hadn't realized how tired she was until this moment.

Except, as a large grey ship came into view, something else became visible.

She blinked, trying to tell if the shape was really who she thought? Her slight frame, still short, but she'd filled out.

Is that my sister?

Nyke's dragon planted a claw on the ground before letting her go. By now she could clearly see it was indeed her sister. Nyke let her go as Lillyanna ran. Her own legs wobbled for a second. Flying wasn't new to her. Flying by dragon however, well. She'd have to get used to that.

"Irene? Is that you," her sister called.

Her legs finally agreed to move when she wanted them too, and she met her sister halfway, and paused.

Lillyanna however did not stop. Irene gasped and tried to cry out as her sister's arms wrapped around her neck. Oh, my God. She was going to kill her. Irene had survived her father, survived a demon attack, saved Nyke, just to be taken out by her sister.

Her heart beat jumped around in her chest. Is this how her life ended?

Calm, mate.

Calm? How could he be so calm. Didn't he care that her sister was going to kill her?

Only as she thought it, the realization that she was still in one piece after several seconds filtered behind the panic. How was this even possible?

Her starving heart didn't care right now that she shouldn't be able to do this. Hug her sister. And she did exactly that. If she was going to die, she'd embrace it just to feel her sister once.

And it was the best feeling ever.

How long had she wanted to feel this? To feel like she wasn't alone in that pit of hell.

"How is this possible," she said, without letting her sister go.

One more squeeze and Lillyanna let go.

"Them. Him," she said, reaching behind her for one more of the massive dragon men. This one wasn't the same as her dragon, though. Where Nyke was all dark and quiet, Lillyanna's dragon was bright and practically beamed with some sort of adolescent excitement.

That was okay. She wasn't sure she could handle Mr. Ray-of-sunshine.

He was right for her sister. She was happy, smiling. Whatever he had done didn't hurt her.

"Lillyanna, what do you mean him? What did he do?"

Lillyanna squeezed her hand. "One, call me Lilly. I like it. And two, let's go inside where we can talk. Maybe you and Nyke want to go rest first?"

Rest? Her head was swimming. The last time she'd seen her sister, she was running for her life into the arms of an alien. The last time she'd seen her sister, she'd honestly had no idea what had happened. Irene had seen a plume of white fire through the trees as she'd been carried away kicking and screaming in her dragon's claws.

The fire had been her sister. Irene had recognized it from the first lab's remains. She recognized it from the training sessions, as her father called them. Really, they were tests and ones that Irene usually came out of feeling sick and exhausted. Tests that Lillyanna, no Lilly, walked away from destroyed. Irene liked the ring of the name Lilly. It seemed to match the beautiful smiling face looking at her.

"Irene, this is a whole new life." Lilly took Irene's hands in her own. "And as much as I still don't have all the answers, it's a life worth living. "

As she stood, a wave of exhaustion flooded her. Irene had been clinging to the anger, the fear, the pain for so long, and now she was suddenly told she could simply release it into the sky and start over.

"Yeah. Maybe I am a little tired, I suppose."

The familiar tingles of magical energy danced along her spine as the warmth of Nyke's arm wrapped itself around her waist. Nyke buried his face into the crook of her neck. "Come, mate. I will take you to our room."

She turned in his arms expecting to kiss him, and he did, but he also lifted her into his arms and walked. She pulled her lips away. "I can walk," she protested.

He grunted and just held her closer.

Stubborn dragon.

Perhaps I am. But, my mate is also tired, and it is my job to protect her, comfort her, please her, and carry her.

He adjusted her in his arms, and she rested her cheek against his warm bare chest.

"I doubt carry is really some kind of rule. But fine. Also, are you naked?" she said.

He chuckled. "Fear not my mate. My brothers aren't concerned by my bare ass."

Someone slapped the back of Nyke's shoulder.

"Speak for yourself. This ass ruins my day pretty regularly."

Irene looked over Nyke's shoulder at one of the others, this one holding the hand of another female she didn't recognize. Curly hair and a beaming smile. The color might have been red, she supposed. The woman waved.

"Kal. Stop. Ignore this idiot. I mean, he's my idiot, but you can ignore him. I'm Maddie. When you're rested, we'll all have time to chat."

Irene looked up into Nyke's face. He was still scowling, but a tick at the corner of his eye said he found the exchange comical.

"See you later, sweet cheeks," called the dragon named Kal. Irene found herself laughing. Honestly laughing for the first time in, well, ever.

Nyke flashed him a gesture that she'd seen a few of the customers at the club give each other and sometimes her when she turned down their offers. She still wasn't clear on what it meant, but she'd assumed it was bad.

It means fuck off on Earth.

She reached up a hand and flicked his pec muscle.

"Stop invading my brain."

Secretly though, or maybe not secretly at all, she was starting to find the odd presence of him comforting.

See, I knew you'd come around.

This time Irene rolled her eyes and just let it go.

yke placed Irene down as they entered his room. Finally, she was safe and away from prying eyes. He wasn't sure how much longer he could handle those men at the club eyeing his mate. The idea of it had him ready to break a few heads. And that was not a good way to stay low profile, not that his dragon cared.

They stood at the door for a few moments as he waited for her to say something. This wasn't as nice as his apartment back home, but it was better than that small room at the club.

Nyke hadn't seen where Irene had grown up, but from Lilly's depictions it wasn't much. More like the cells they used for their own prisoners.

He wanted to give her so much more. Glimpses of images flashed through her mind and he tried to make heads or tails of them. Even being in her head, he still didn't understand his female. Sad memories closely followed by images of him. The scent of fear would come and go as quickly as he blinked. He finally understood what his brothers were complaining about.

For several moments she remained quiet. Nyke wanted to respect her, not breaking into her mind all the time, but he was dying to know what she thought. This had to be better? It was better than the room she currently called home. If only she'd have embraced him sooner, they could have avoided so many things, like that horrible job.

Flexing his fingers into fists, he tried to squeeze out the frustration of any man seeing her with her ass nearly hanging out. He hated how those tops didn't fit her curves, and he could barely believe she could stay in half of them. The cotton PJ's she currently wore, he didn't mind much. Or rather, he hated them the most. The electric buzz jumping from him to her and the need to strip her down naked blinded his logic.

He loved the idea of seeing her in his bed, wrapped within his arms.

She seemed so engulfed in her thoughts she didn't notice him until he placed a kiss on the side of her neck.

The intake of breath as he ran his hand along her stomach, the exact reaction he hoped for.

When she finally looked up, he still couldn't read her.

"Well? What do you think?"

She said nothing. Just looked at him. He pressed into her, and she shivered against him.

"Are you cold, mate?" Nyke asked.

Irene shook her head. "No, never with you."

Pushing up on her tiptoes, her face upturned to his. She kissed him, softly. He'd behaved for far too long. He needed his mate.

Pulling in her scent, he growled.

"Mm. Mate, you smell delicious."

Her fingers splayed over his chest.

Nyke let himself enjoy the moment. His moment where he finally had his mate within his clutches. He'd known she was out there, but until he'd scented her in that underground shit hole, he wasn't convinced he wanted a mate. No. He hadn't wanted the headache.

Kal, Eadric, and Deo could have their complicated life. But now? Now, he couldn't get enough of her.

Complicated or not, he didn't want his life any other way.

It was his turn to erase her past fears. Erase a past that scared her and tormented her. A past that had nothing to do with him and he couldn't do a thing about except help her forget.

"Mate, are you happy?"

She remained silent as her fingers played against his bare chest.

He stroked her back, loving how she seemed to purr at every stroke.

He wanted to massage away her fears, kiss away her sadness.

It seemed like whenever he left her mind to its own devices, it circled back to something awful. He still couldn't see everything, not yet. But he hated how she tried to shield the dark spots in her mind.

"I am happy. I don't even think that word can sum up what I feel."

The beautiful scent of her body caught his attention as her warm, soft lips kissed his chest.

"I feel safe," she whispered.

She kissed the opposite pec next. "I feel less alone."

She kissed a little higher and every time her beautiful lips left him, she left a trail of fire that made him nearly purr in satisfaction.

"I feel loved," she said, before he cradled her chin between his fingers and claimed her lips.

Her words circled his mind, and finally he found the right one to explain it all.

Complete.

She started to pull away, but he wouldn't let her. Her lips belonged on his.

You feel complete, because you complete me. I love you.

A fragmented thought of him lifting her made him smile

against her lips. She would get better at this communication, but for now that was enough.

Gripping her beautiful full ass, he lifted her and made the last few strides to his bed.

Slowly, he lowered her to the soft surface. His body hovered over her as he bent forward and gripped the waistband of her sleep shorts.

"You have entirely too many clothes on right now," he grumbled.

She giggled. "And you have far too few on in front of those other women."

Nyke rarely felt the need to smile, but with his mate he couldn't help it.

"Jealousy?" he asked.

Her cheeks flushed pink. "No. Why would I be jealous?"

He shrugged and continued to pull at her shorts.

"Precisely. You have no reason."

She squirmed as his fingers grazed her thighs, and then her calves before he pulled the fabric away and tossed it behind him.

"Really? No reason? How would you feel if I danced in front of those guys out there?" she said.

Nyke stopped with his hands resting on her knees. "My brothers?"

She nibbled her lower lip, looking up at him.

"You will never walk in front of any male unclothed. I've had to watch you flaunt yourself in front of men for far too long and as for me, it is impossible in moments like this. You need not worry though, the females have eyes only for their mates."

The way she watched him made him feel bare. He hadn't been kidding when he'd told her she saved him.

"You're glowing," she said.

Lowering his lips to her leg, he kissed his way up. "We have an eternity to talk. No more words, mate."

His hands slid up the naked skin along her thighs. "The only noise I want to hear from you are your screams of pleasure as I lick every inch of your body."

His thumbs brushed the sensitive v between her legs, and she squirmed.

"Mine," he growled. His mouth claimed her mouth as he buried his finger inside her, finding that sensitive spot between her legs and making her squirm in need. He swallowed her gasps as he stroked her. The thump of her heartbeat increased as he slipped a second finger in. His rhythm increasing. He needed her to come for him. He needed her to forget everything except him.

Dropping his lips to her breasts, he took her nipple between his teeth. Gently nipping at the peak. Nyke smiled as her body reacted to the added sensation. Her core quaked around his fingers.

Kissing her lips, he waited for her breathing to even out.

"Are you ready for more, mate?"

Her eyes glazed over in lust as he positioned his dick between her legs. He pressed against her slick heat and nearly groaned as her tight muscles stretched around him.

He let out a hiss of air as he controlled his own need. Slowly retreating before pressing further. Her nails bit into his shoulders as he drove deeper and deeper until he was fully seated.

"You feel so good," he said, whispering against her ear as he found a rhythm. Her hips rocked against his as he pushed in again and again, claiming her lips as her breathing grew ragged.

Yes, in this moment there was just them. Just the two of them.

"I love you," she said on a breath.

The love that filled her bled through their connection. He claimed her lips once more, thrusting once, twice, three times until her body pulsed around him, taking from him everything as he let his own release go.

He would give her anything. Everything. She was his mate. She completed him.

* * *

Nyke woke in a sweat. Laying in bed, he ran his hands through his hair.

What the fuck was in his head?

He felt around and found the beautiful frame of Irene next to him. She tossed and turned. His lips pressed into a thin line. They were her nightmares.

There was no need to wake her. She needed to rest. He loved watching her sleep, but right now as he watched her, his heart constricted in worry. Her eyes flitted behind her lids and her brow furrowed. Sadness and fear scented the room. This wasn't right. She should be happy here. He would protect her always.

He pulled her into the crook of his body and the anxiety pulsing through their connection slowed. Nyke second guessed looking into her thoughts. He wanted to help her calm her mind. Hesitation took hold as he studied her still figure. Not only was he certain he didn't want to see what was going on in her head, he wasn't sure she'd be okay sharing this part of her past.

The dark visions in his head were definitely from her past. The goddess knew he had plenty of his own demons, but these weren't his.

A few seconds ticked by and her heart rate slowed, her breathing became even, and the tension in her forehead eased. He'd let her keep these secrets. If she didn't want to share, he understood. Everyone had a past they weren't proud of. Everyone had a past.

Sleep didn't come back. Part of him couldn't release the dark images. How could he help her forget an entire lifetime? Perhaps she needed more time with her sister? He'd make note of that for later.

Nyke rubbed the back of his neck. He couldn't tell if they were a dream or a memory. Dozens of faces. Some cried, others pleaded. It made him sick. Her father was a monster. Images of what he assumed were souls, ghosts maybe, smiling and flying away replaced the horrible visions. Nyke believed in the soul, his dragon was his very essence. But he'd never seen one leave its body behind like that. Strange how her mind worked.

Nyke ran his hand over her shoulder. They'd lay in each other's arms for hours, and at least here the bed was big enough he didn't feel any reason to move.

Her words broke the comfortable silence. "So when do we leave?"

His finger traced lazy circles over her skin. "Leave for where?"

Shifting, she looked over her shoulder. "Leave for your planet."

A smile touched his lips. She was ready to return home with him. Perhaps he'd gotten the easiest mate so far. Thank the goddess.

He placed a kiss on her temple. "We will leave soon, mate. As soon as my brothers are all ready. Let's sleep for a few more hours and then we can discuss this with the others."

She rolled over, her fingers running a trail down his chest to his abs. The sensations shooting straight down to his dick.

"I'm not in the mood for sleep. Perhaps you can help me forget my nightmares instead?" Her lips gently kissed his chest and her hand cupped his balls.

What had she just asked him? He smirked as he rolled her over and spread her legs with his knee.

"Whatever you say, Angel."

13

*I*rene woke with a start, punching something heavy and hard laying atop her.

As the object moved, it let out a loud swear. "Fuck, what was that for?"

Her eyes adjusted to the dark of the room as she sat up. The large figure next to her rubbing his shoulder came into focus.

"Oh. Sorry." Was all she could think to say. "I, I uh, had a bad dream."

His large hand wrapped around her arm and pulled her closer, and she didn't fight it.

"Well, whoever it was in that bad dream would regret coming after you. That's going to leave a mark."

She gave a shrug. "Sorry. I didn't mean to hurt you."

His chest vibrated as he chuckled. "You didn't exactly hurt me, more like surprised the shit out of me while I was dreaming of you. At least I still woke up to your beautiful body."

Her heart still beat like the wings of a trapped insect. She knew where she was, her brain knew where she was, but something was wrong. No, not wrong. Memories. Her memories were a bitch.

"My sister?"

Nyke folded her into his body.

"She is safe, with my brother."

Right. She was safe. Irene was safe. But something was wrong. Something in her wouldn't settle down.

"What time is it?"

Nyke called out to something in a language she hadn't heard.

A shiver chased her spine at his commanding voice. Maybe she could get him to talk to her like that later.

"It is four p.m. mountain standard earth time," said a pleasant sounding female voice.

"What is that?" she asked.

"Our ship's AI. She responds to commands, but we are limited to how. Mine won't respond to English, yet. I tried having something more advanced, but she would go off and start playing music at the worst times. Still, she's mostly limited to the bridge these days. It's four. Did that answer your question?"

She shifted against him. "I don't know. Something is wrong. I feel off."

He nuzzled her neck. "The only thing wrong is that you aren't sleeping. You are safe, mate. Lay down and sleep with me."

She pushed away, sliding to the edge of the bed.

"No. I can't sleep and if I have sex with you one more time, I won't be walking out of here on my own. Still, I just can't shake this feeling. I don't know what to think."

Nyke moved, shaking the bed next to her as he settled behind her.

"It was just a nightmare. The feeling, it was from that nightmare."

She cracked her knuckles and flexed her fingers.

"It wasn't just a nightmare." Irene wanted to forget it. He was right. Whatever had happened to her head was why she couldn't shake this feeling.

What was it that bugged her the most? She raised her hands and pressed them against her temples.

"Irene, I can see the fragments in your memory. It was a nightmare. You are safe here. Your sister is safe."

Yes, her sister was. But nothing else alive was. She tried to remember the nightmare. The dark hallway. Where had she seen it before? Why had she seen it before?

Where was it from?

"Nyke, has anyone else been rescued from my father's labs? Or just my sister and I?"

He was quiet for a moment and as much as she wanted to know what he was thinking, she could barely focus on the mess in her own thoughts.

"Well, there was one woman rescued when we got Deo back. But no one else. Is that who you mean?"

She shook her head.

"No, I don't think so. It's like a part of my memory isn't work-ing. I can tell there is something there that I should know, but I can't seem to recall it."

"How can I help?"

The heat of his warm body comforted her, but it still didn't push away the nagging dark figure from her dream. There was someone else there, someone she felt was important.

"You can read my mind right?" she asked.

Nyke kissed the top of her head. "Yes, but I won't ever do anything without your permission."

She could feel the truth in his words, the truth of everything he believed. She didn't have to be proficient in reading his mind. His emotions were clear to her. The purity of his heart a beacon in her own dark soul.

"Can you see if," she paused. See what? She wasn't even sure what she was asking him to do. Break into her mind? Yes. But what was he looking for? Did she want to know if she was a monster? Or was one of the rescued souls she freed lurking somewhere in her own soul? Maybe she was asking him to tell her if she was crazy. Maybe she'd lead with that.

"Can you look in my mind and tell me what you see? From my dream?"

"Turn around and look at me?" he asked.

She did as told, closing her eyes as she turned to face him. She didn't want to look into his eyes, the pools of swirling blue and purple that brought her to her knees. She didn't want them to see through her, and she was most afraid that he would see her inner demon. Not the kind of demons her father controlled. One all her own. One that scared her so much, because she couldn't kill it and run from it. It was who she was deep down inside and there was no rescue from yourself.

What if she was everything she hated? Only Nyke didn't give her that feeling. He didn't let her hide.

The heat of his hand on her cheek subdued the self-destructive bomb of her own hatred.

"Look at me, my angel," he commanded.

She couldn't refuse him, even if she didn't want to see him look at her differently. After he'd seen who she really was, would he still see her the same? She'd already spent her life being hated. Treated like a lab rat when all else failed. She couldn't bear it if he hated her.

She gasped out a sob before even knowing her own heartbreak.

"Irene, what's wrong?" Nyke's voice grew concerned as he pulled her into a hug that was almost too tight. She welcomed the suffocating feeling of being loved, because at the end of the day or week or year, she had finally felt love unconditionally returned.

"Tell me what is wrong, mate. I can't fix what I don't understand."

She sniffled. "I can't bear the idea of losing you."

Gently, he pulled her away from his chest. Embarrassment

couldn't even break through her pain as she saw the trail of tears down his shoulder.

"You will not lose me. What has brought this on?"

She placed a hand on either side of his face, trying to calm herself as she looked deep into the soul of her beautiful savior. "I need you to see what is in my head that I can't. I need to know what I can't remember and if you see something you shouldn't, I'm afraid that you will turn me away."

Nyke's beautiful full lips spread into a smile as his hands met hers.

"There is nothing I could see that would change my love for you. Perhaps fate has chosen us to be together for some larger purpose, but I have chosen you for myself. I can feel the good in your soul and I can hear the strength of your heart. There is nothing on this planet or the next that could make me ever feel any less for you."

Her breath hitched as the gravity of his words sank in. He loved her. She knew this. Of course she did. Maybe she should have thought to hear the finality of the words before giving her body to him, but she'd already seen it in his actions. In every glance. She'd seen it in every kiss and touch. But to hear those words. The words she'd longed to hear since her childhood. The words whispered in every book she snuck in to read. The words she never knew she wanted to hear, to suddenly not feel alone.

"I love you too," she whispered, as if saying them too loud would make this any less real. "Then can you help me?"

"Yes, or maybe not. But I will try. Now tell me where to start."

She spread her legs, aware of her nakedness as she straddled his lap. She needed to be close to him, hold on to him as an anchor.

"I don't really know. I thought maybe you would know how to do this better?"

He placed a gentle kiss on the top of her nose.

"I know a bit about connections with my brothers, but we've

never trained for locked memories. Perhaps you start with the last clear memory you have that you know is real? The one before the time that you feel is missing?"

Irene nodded. She turned her face up to his, closing her eyes and leaving herself to his mercy.

She relaxed as his lips covered hers in a gentle kiss that sent a wave of comfort through her. Allowing her to clear her mind of anything but him and the one solid memory of sadness that had no real connection to anything. No reason but a dark tunnel. A tunnel she dreamed of over and over and over again.

Open your mind to me, Nyke prodded.

She did, or rather she tried. She wanted to invite him in, if that was a thing.

Her body shivered and then relaxed at the welcome invasion. It was strange feeling him in her mind. She could feel his dragon clearly now. Here, in her mind, he was stripped raw. Nothing hidden.

She could suddenly feel everything he felt, and she was sure that he could feel her.

Focus, Irene.

Right. He was here for a reason. She needed to help him.

Clearing her mind of everything except for the last memory she could remember, of her standing in a dark hall that she couldn't place. She remembered being somewhere near this place, if it was a place. Was the missing memory creating this strange void, or was the strange void all that was left of the memory?

The walls of her mental barrier didn't flex at the invasion. No, instead they tried to splinter and crack as her dragon tried to cram his too large body into the space. She clenched her teeth at the pain. Maybe the lock to the forgotten place in her mind was there, only a few more memories. But, no. The harder he pushed the more her mind split, and it suddenly felt like he was standing on one side of her mind and on the other side was a hidden room. She knew even if he could find the entrance it would break her.

She started to sweat. No. Whatever was there scared her. No. No. No.

Nyke pushed against the wall once more and she couldn't take it anymore. She let herself scream against the pain.

Seconds or maybe it was hours passed before she could refocus on the feel of Nyke's warmth against her shoulders.

Her chest burned, liked she'd just run a mile or two. Her head throbbed, and it took her a few more seconds to realize Nyke was calling her name.

"Irene? Come back to me," he called.

The light burned as she blinked. It had been too dark where she'd been locked away in her brain.

"Do you remember anything?" Nyke asked.

She shook her head and instantly regretted the motion.

"No. But my head hurts like someone just hit me."

Nyke grunted. "Whatever they did to you isn't something I know how to work with. It's like the memory isn't even there. I couldn't see anything and I could feel myself pushing you too hard. Are you alright?"

A curt nod of her head and she started to shake her head. No. She always said she was, but really. "No. No. I'm not okay. My father has been messing with more than just my life, he did something to my memories. I always thought that being his daughter, I was safe. Or, well, safe enough. He always thought I was powerless, nearly useless if it weren't for my ability to help with his experiments as he called them."

Nyke wrapped her into him.

"It's okay. You're safe here."

She shook her head. "I'm not safe if we are here. You're not safe. My father never gives up. When do we leave?"

Irene never saw herself leaving this life, this hell on Earth. But finally there was a light. This was all going to end soon. And it was all she could picture.

His hand traced a line down her spine in a repetitive motion, calming a panic that didn't want to be hushed right now.

"We will leave as soon as my brothers all find their mates."

She drew in a breath against the tightness in her chest.

"How many more are there? Brothers, that is? To mate?"

She tried to let the motion of his fingers calm her.

"Two. There are two more of us that have not claimed their mate."

Claimed? That was a good sign, right?

"Claimed? So they know who they are? Can they just do the mating thing? I'll talk to the women. Tell them it's good. Totally worth doing. Where are they?"

She slid back, intent on getting up.

"Just good? The mating thing? I suppose I am pleased you think it was worth it. You are only bound to me in soul and body." Nyke's enormous hands wrapped around her hips, pulling her down.

"You know what I mean, Nyke. I mean I can explain to them they just need to embrace it even if they aren't sure yet. I can explain that they will never fill this invisible hole they probably didn't even know they had until they accept their dragon."

Nyke's lip twitched. "You are not making this sound any better, mate."

She glared. "Nyke, please just let me go hurry this process up. I need to get off this planet."

Only, as she said the words, they seemed wrong. Selfish. And like a mistake.

"I can't let you go and hurry the process up as you so eloquently put it. Only one of my brothers has seen his mate. The other has no idea where his mate still is."

She gave up her fight.

"Oh."

A gentle kiss warmed her cheek.

"We will find his mate soon enough and for now, you are safe here. With me. I would not allow anyone or anything to hurt you."

She knew this. She knew he would never hurt her. She'd seen it that night one of her father's things had tried to come for her. She'd seen her future in his giant dragon eyes. Safety. Comfort. Love.

Even in those few scary moments where she could feel him, feel his soul, she'd already been his. Something deep inside her knew him, and she needed him more than she needed her next breath.

She also needed to figure how to take her next breath with a weight heavy on her chest. She had everything, and yet she needed something else.

"Can we go back to the club, one last time?"

14

"Let me get this straight, your mate thinks I should go with you to an establishment that is like a bar only with naked women? Why does she think my mate will be there?"

Nyke shrugged. "It couldn't hurt. When was the last time you even tried to find your mate?"

Cy curled his lip. "You're a real asshole sometimes, Nyke."

Barak shook his head. "We don't have time for you to be picky, Cy, maybe Nyke has a point. Maybe you aren't trying hard enough."

Nyke watched as Cy's dragon flashed in his eyes. "Calm yourself. I never said you weren't trying. I asked when was the last time you'd gone to find her? All the other mates have presented themselves when we least expect. Perhaps this is your chance?"

Barak suddenly stood. "I'll help, best I can. But I need to get back to my own problems soon. Just call me when you're ready to head out."

They both watched as Barak practically ran off. He had his own uphill battle, but Nyke knew he could count on him to help protect his mate. Nyke ran his hands through his hair. Fuck, after seeing the issues each of them had had with each mate, they all feared why Cy hadn't yet seen his mate. Barak's mate was going to be one of the hardest to overcome. He hated to ask him for help, but Nyke knew he would. They all would do anything they could for each other.

Now he just had to get Cy on board with Irene's plan. Irene seemed insistent that they at least try to find him a mate. The tension rolled off her like a rope that was wound too tight; it threatened to fray.

Irene insisted they find Cy his mate. Nyke knew she was at her limit when she'd suggest something short of kidnapping Barak's. Nyke could feel the fear within her. The only time he ever felt her calm was when he made love to her, but even he couldn't stay in bed forever.

Someday he'd have to go back to protecting the galaxies. Someday he'd be home and things would be back to normal, or as normal as a soldier ever got. Their mate's would be left to console each other and become a support group when the warriors were called upon.

Nyke had left Irene in the care of the other mates, one being her sister. He hoped it would settle her mind. He fucking hated that something haunted her and he couldn't seem to chase it away. He could see it in her face, in her eyes. Irene had hidden the extent of her fear even through their connection, and he hated it. She shouldn't want to hide anything from him.

"Cy, just try it. When was the last time you left this ship? It's not healthy."

Cy glared. "I left the last time I had to save one of your asses. Every fucking time someone leaves or finds their mate, some-thing blows up in our face. It's like the goddess is punishing us to figure out something. I hate her fucking games."

This had been a trip designed in hell. Irony not lost on them that somehow demons existed on Earth rather than remaining within their own dimensions. The dragon warriors were not strangers to strange creatures, aliens that had found their way to other dimensions through wormholes, black holes, and dark magic that defied all known logic. The issue was, Earth was supposed to be a haven. The only magic here was supposed to be minor, even benign.

Stories of Earth through thousands of years said it was slow to develop. Magic wasn't born here, but rather was because of species meddling. Some species had been allowed to remain here, learning to integrate into human societies. Nyke studied cultures from across the galaxies in order to know the best way to plan for a battle plan. And yet, demon magic? This hadn't been reported on Earth the last time a scouting party had visited.

"Nyke, what do you think of your bride now?" asked Maddie, as the mates giggled and came into the commons area where Cy and Nyke sat.

He turned as he felt her presence.

He pursed his lips. "Why is that stuff on her face? She was beautiful before."

He tried to hide his cringe. His mate looked hot and his dick instantly reacted. But then again, he struggled to control himself regardless of what she wore.

"Don't you dare judge her makeup? She looks hot and you know it, Nyke. Irene, you've got a lot of work with this one. Mr. Serious-pants," scowled Maddie.

Irene laughed, but walked over and wrapped her hands around his bicep. "I can handle him just fine."

A moment later his brothers came in, each grabbing up their mate in greeting. The sadness rolling off of Cy stopped them in their tracks. Their connection as a unit was just as strong as each of their connections to their mates. The difference was, when one of them was hurting or happy, it would broadcast to all of them.

"Cy, you know I'm right. Let's try something different."

Nyke didn't add to the reality that although he actually did hope Cy might find her, he wanted his mate to calm. If it gave her hope to take him out he was on board. Nyke didn't hold on to the idea that they would get off this rock any faster.

"So, what's the plan? Are we going to a strip club tonight?" Maddie asked.

Kal grabbed her up in his arms and Nyke no longer felt the insane jealousy he'd once felt at his brother's happiness. Still, for Cy's sake, Nyke refused to display his happiness as freely. Besides, it wasn't lost on him. If he smiled now, he'd set up a new expectation. Not, happening.

"Mate, I am the only stripper you need. Shall I take you back to bed and give you a private showing?" Kal teased, nipping at Maddie.

Lilly pecked Eadric's cheek as she left her mate to come sit by Irene.

"I want to come with you. See where you've been living," Lilly said.

Eadric rolled his eyes, but nodded.

"Deo, what is your choice? Is your mate better off here? With the demon activity, I would feel better if perhaps you and Aisha stayed here while we went back for Irene to say farewell."

He glanced back at his mate. "You are sure you must go back?"

Irene nodded and when she turned up her bright beautiful eyes that swirled with shades of blue and golden flecks, he couldn't say no.

"I really need to say thank you to Ruby. Also, we really need to find Cy his mate."

She glanced over to Cy and smiled. "I prefer to take care of people, just ask my sister."

Cy groaned. "How can I say no to that?"

Nyke chuckled and his brother paused a moment as if the sound were foreign. Eh, maybe it was. So what? They'd have to get used to him being happy, or well happier at least when his Irene was around.

"So it's settled. Barak and Cy will come. Eadric you will bring

Lilly and at the first sign of trouble you will be in charge of her. Truthfully, Lilly might be a good defense in case daddy dearest shows himself again."

Irene's hands chilled against his skin. He tried to reach through their connection but she'd somehow mastered blocking him out already, or at least she was good at shielding her emotions.

Mate, you are okay?

She nodded.

"Alright. Let's go. It's close to opening." He turned to Irene. "You won't be able to work, though. This is your chance to say goodbye, and that is all."

She nodded again. He couldn't put his finger on it, but Nyke assumed once she was back here she would calm and talk. He hated not knowing what was going through her head right now. That wasn't how mates were supposed to work.

"Mate, are you sure you're okay? You keep blocking me."

His own senses screamed that this would not go as planned. No, when the hell did it ever go as planned.

Irene's fingers played along the skin on his arm. He didn't mind the contact, but he hated her hesitation.

"Yeah. I think so. I just need to say goodbye, I think."

Nyke didn't like her being uncertain. It was obvious that she wasn't going to give him more either.

"Fine, let's meet outside in ten minutes. Deo and Kal, we will be in contact. This should be simple. And with any luck Cy will find his mate."

* * *

Nyke's bare feet scratched against the dead underbrush of their latest location. Anything was better than the sand pit called a desert. Here, though, there wasn't room enough for them to all take off at once.

He struggled to differentiate the tension leaching from Irene and what might have been his own apprehension of the night. Nothing had been going to plan echoed around his head.

He cradled Irene's hand as he led her out to the clearing where Cy stood in dragon form, his head hanging.

Brother, you alright?

The dragon snorted in response.

"Is that Cy?" Irene asked.

Nyke nodded. "Yeah. I think he's just trying not to get his hopes up. The search for our mates has been wearing on each of us and to be the last is hard."

I can hear you fuck-stick, screamed Cy through their connection.

Nyke let his lips twitch in amusement. He was still in there, at least.

"Alight mate. Climb on," Nyke said, as he took a few more steps and shifted.

His dragon stretched his wings, enjoying the freedom.

This would be fine. All would be okay; he extended his foreleg and helped Irene hoist herself up. The dragon sniffed the air, breathing in the scent of his mate.

"I know what you're doing, Nyke. Calm your dang self. It's like you're never satisfied," Irene teased.

His dragon's chest rumbled at her comment. She wasn't wrong though.

How can I help it? My mate is everything I'd ever wanted.

Once her ass was firmly seated on the scruff of his long neck, he felt her lean forward into him. A hug, he supposed, for lack of a better description. His dragon loved the attention, and he loved that their mate was safe with them.

Here comes Eadric. Barak is already airborne.

Okay, then we're going? Irene responded.

Cy took off at that very second. In a quick flurry, he turned and pushed off with his back legs. The wind whipped around them and he felt Irene's thighs squeeze tighter and he adjusted his angle. Once he was up in the air flying alongside his brothers, he tried to shake the feeling that they weren't just heading back to say goodbye.

Anyone else feel that?

A few moments of silence.

The magic in the air sours my stomach. Something bad is coming. Eadric answered.

Cy turned and flew ahead. Nyke waited for his report before he bothered saying anything to Irene. None of this was right.

Perhaps we abort the plan? Cy said a few minutes later.

Nyke reached for his mate's mind. How are you?

The fidget of her fingers against his hide belied her next words.

Fine. Just looking forward to saying thank you to Ruby. Do you think Cy could really find his mate this easily?

Nyke had no idea, but she seemed hopeful. *We've all found our mates when we least expected it. I never imagined finding you in a hole in the ground.*

The heat of her body rested against him as she hugged him tighter.

I know. I never expected to find someone to love me, not in a million years.

The sound of her words hurt, even if he had come for her. Found her. And protected her while he could, the fact anyone could be so devoid of love in their life, especially his mate, broke him. Even in the worst of their days as warriors, even when they lose someone, they are never alone. They have families and those that no longer do they have their brothers. Nyke had been training with the same group since childhood. They knew how the others worked almost better than they knew themselves.

Perhaps growing up knowing what you're destined for wasn't how most societies lived, but it worked for him. He knew who he was, knew where he would go someday, knew who was here for him, and most importantly he'd always had his brothers.

No one should feel that way ever, Mate. You are worth loving.

He banked right as the currents of air ebbed and flowed.

Almost there. The others are uneasy. Let's make this quick.

He didn't wait for her response as they touched down on the roof of the brick building he'd become well acquainted with.

As Irene got off, Nyke shifted and headed for an outcropping where he stashed what he considered to be a human survival kit.

He tossed pants at his brothers and t-shirts. That should pass well enough.

Irene started down the fire escape.

"Irene, wait for us?" he asked, his head popping through the neckline of the shirt.

"I'm just taking Lilly to my room. We will wait for you inside."

He grunted.

Looking at his brothers, he nodded at them. "I don't have enough boots for each of us. Perhaps Eadric and Barak, you stay up here as a lookout?"

Both nodded, except Eadric reached for a duffle next to him. "My mate left this for me. It's a few more changes of clothes and shoes." Shuffling through it, he pulled out a pair of shoes and another. "Three pair? Perhaps the females know more than we give them credit for?"

Nyke shrugged. "We really need to stop underestimating them. All we ever do is get proven wrong. Anything else in that bag that might be helpful?"

Eadric dug around and pulled out some additional clothing, a few snacks, a knife, and two sets of female clothing. "My mate was apparently ready for just about anything. There's a flashlight and first aid kit as well."

Cy didn't smile when he spoke. "Well, at least she appears to know you, or maybe I should say us. We attack trouble like fucking sharks to blood."

Nyke nodded. "Let's go. My mate needs closure and we need to get out of here. Cy, go sniff around and see if anyone catches your eye."

One by one they slid down the ladder to Irene's room, climbing in through the window. The familiar thump of the base from downstairs vibrated the floor.

He couldn't wait to be done with this place.

Irene walked around her room. There was nothing to take. Nothing was hers. Even the clothing had been cast offs from other girls. It was okay, though. This place held few memories, and all of them were better than her entire past. Here was the first time she'd realized she could love someone. Clasping her hands loosely in front of her, she shrugged.

"We can go as soon as Nyke says it's okay," Irene said.

Irene flinched as Lilly laid her hand on her shoulder.

"Don't worry, sister. I won't hurt you, I promise."

Irene glanced over her shoulder and studied her sister's hand. She raised her hand only to pull it back. Slowly, she allowed herself to reach for her sister. As her hand settled on Lilly's, Irene let out a sob. Never in a million years would she have thought she would stand in the outside world, but not only was she in the outside world, she was touching her sister.

Without thinking, she turned and pulled Lilly into her arms.

"You have no idea how many years I've wanted to do this," she whispered.

Lilly hugged her back as they just stood there for several

moments. Irene wiped at the tears she couldn't control, letting out a laugh as Lilly pulled away.

"I would have welcomed a hug. I'm so glad that the goddess has a much better plan for you than father."

A chill sent goosebumps across her body. "Right. Father."

Something in the air wasn't right. A churning in her stomach displacing the happiness. She still couldn't shake that something was still off. She needed to fix this before they could leave.

Looking around the room, she closed this door in her heart. She would not be a sitting duck here anymore. If anything, she'd learned these last few days is that she couldn't hide. Not here anyway. Maybe not anywhere on this planet.

It was okay.

Two large figures climbed through the window. It was time to move on. It was time to move into an unknown future. For once, the unknown was comfortable. She'd grown up knowing history books and stories never shared the actual truth about Earth. She was okay leaving behind the Illuminati. For all their theories and their stories, they never seemed to break into society. Her father seemed to resent that. She would not pay the price for his unhappiness anymore, though.

Irene led them out of her room. She really wished she could stop her father once and for all. A side effect of feeling was that she wasn't just starting to understand love. No, she was starting to understand the darkness, hate. The feeling for her father was hate.

Anger boiled in her veins as they walked down the hall. How is it that she'd been so deprived of everything that she had thought this place was an upgrade? It was run down, smelled, and there was no peace during club hours. But it had been hers. The fact that her life had been devoid of so many things that this had been a luxury pissed her off.

Irene tried to clear her head. Her hands were shaking as anger filled her the more memories did and didn't surface. Everything had been because her father envied power and even now he'd done something to her, taken memories just so he could keep power over her.

Someone like him didn't deserve to run freely when his hate spread like a disease.

"Mate, are you alright?"

"I will be," she said.

She let out a breath and allowed the warmth of Nyke to fill her. What was he? Mate. Yes, was there another word for him? He was her world, her future. There had to be something more than a mate. She wasn't a shifter; she was something human. She thought. Her sister was definitely part demon, maybe a witch? Demonic magic mixed into the human race. Is that what Irene was? A witch? Even now, she didn't exactly know how she fit into her future.

Nyke wrapped his arm around her, gently pulling her to face him. "Do not lie. I feel you in here." He pointed to his chest. "Remember?"

Irene allowed a small smile. She remembered. "I do." Reaching up she kissed him. A gentle kiss, but one that said thank you. He would challenge her, but he wasn't pushing her. He never had.

"Like, I said. I will be. Let's go downstairs and find Ruby. I can't leave her. She protected me from what she could. She gave me a room, and food, and a job. She was kind. That deserves a thanks."

She left the apartment with four gigantic men ducking to get through the doorframe and her sister.

Nyke reached for the door, "Let me."

Her hand let it go. This was new. Being taken care of and it almost made her uncomfortable.

"Thanks."

Everyone was quiet, not that it would have mattered with the club directly below them. She'd always thought it had been dumb to put rooms above such a place, but then again it wasn't like the area was all that nice.

A few moments later, they walked into the back of the club.

"Alright. Fan out. Cy, do what you need while I take Irene to find Ruby. Eadric and Barak, you look out for anything strange. We don't need any more surprises."

Barak seemed to almost laugh. "When have we not had surprise after surprise lately?"

Irene shivered even though the club was warm. Stale alcohol, the familiar perfume in this place. She still hesitated. Her sister was close, her mate was by her side. They could handle anything. That last attack had left her uneasy. Her father knew where she was. Maybe it had been dumb to come back.

Blowing out a breath, she steadied her nerves. She would feel better once they got out of here.

Dumb or not, her conscience wouldn't let her rest if she left Ruby without a clue of what happened. She couldn't just walk away.

She rubbed at her arms, and Nyke pulled her close.

"Ruby is usually at the front," she said. Nyke nodded and followed. He gave her confidence when she felt unsure. Was she making the right choice? Leaving? Maybe saying goodbye to Ruby would fix the doubt growing like an avalanching snowball in her stomach.

She wanted Nyke and all that he promised, but with each step towards Ruby her throat grew a hair tighter Saying goodbye was apparently hard when you actually had someone to be thankful for.

"There, she's near a table," Nyke said, as he pointed.

She turned and corrected her path. Here went nothing and yet everything she'd known. Sad that she hadn't lived until these last few days. A week for her was her entire life, because she hadn't once lived while in that lab.

"You have to tell her you are leaving too. You were like the best bouncer we've had since I got here."

His hand snaked around her waist, and he gave her hip a squeeze. "I would do anything I needed to keep my mate safe."

His words seeped into her and helped ease the boulders of doubt and unease that seemed to still want to plant themselves deep in her gut. Yeah, no, she wasn't getting around this, but at least Nyke helped.

Mostly.

Wringing her hands, she stopped behind Ruby, who's hands were still animatedly flying around causing Irene to duck.

"Oh, I wasn't expecting you back," said Ruby, as she turned around.

Doubt filled the remainder of space in her gut. "Why? I couldn't not say goodbye."

Ruby flashed a bright red smile, the crow's feet at the corner of her eyes easy to see even in the dim lighting with strobe and stage lights flashing.

Irene realized she wished she'd been around a little longer to hear all of Ruby's story. She'd been the closest thing to a mom Irene had ever known, even if it was only for a short time.

Ruby shrugged. "I figured there was more to you than you let on. Besides, no one like him comes to hang around places like this. As long as he isn't the reason you were under my stairs."

Irene shook her head. "No, no. He is the reason I got out of my old life. I was just too far in to realize what was right in front of me."

"Oh little girl, I have seen my fair share of abuse and toxic relationships to know. He was far too protective of you and you were too relaxed. I watched him. I watched you. Why do you think I hired him on? To keep an eye on him, of course," Ruby said, hands on her hips.

Irene blinked away a prick of tears. All this time she'd just figured Ruby gave a down-on-her-luck girl a job. She had no idea why she'd hired Nyke, other than he was certainly eye candy for the dancers. A stir of jealousy pitted itself against the dread already trying to take over.

Nyke was her's, not anyone else's.

Mate, you are okay? he asked.

She gave a quick glance up at him, trying to hide the heat in her cheeks.

Fine. Why would you ask that?

He gave her a knowing look. She turned her eyes down. So what if he knew she was jealous? Still unsure of herself. She'd just met the guy.

Mate, you are my soul. There is no other for me. He knew exactly what she needed to hear to get past all her doubts. It could take years for her to overcome all the damage her father had created. But, with each moment, each glance, he was healing each one.

"I know Ivy, I know. You go live your best life."

Ruby's eyes flicked over to Nyke. "I suppose this means you aren't sticking around either then. Humph. Figures. Ivy deserves the best, and while I'm not sure you're the best, you sure look the part."

Irene looked up in time to see Nyke scowl. She stifled a giggle.

You're the best, she's just joking. Deep breath, Nyke.

His eyes met hers. Perhaps he could hide his emotions in public, but she could see the amusement in his eyes.

Irene turned back to Ruby. "Thank you again for everything, for showing me what it was like to matter. "

Irene leaned forward and wrapped her arms around Ruby. She nearly pulled away as she realized what she was doing. What was she doing? But when Ruby reached around her she realized that this was okay. Touching someone was okay.

"Before you go, there have been several men looking for you today. Be careful?"

Irene shared a glance with Nyke.

"What did these males look like?" asked Nyke.

Ruby shrugged. "I'll do you one better than a description. Sometimes I try to keep my friends close and my enemies closer. They gave off a real bad vibe. I put them over in that corner, far from the stage, and have been watching them."

They all turned to look at a booth that was pretty much useless for customers because it had obstructed views of just about the entire place. Right now, though, it stood empty.

"Hm, they were just there. Well, there were three. Vacant looking eyes and they just kept repeating themselves. I said if you got nothing else to say to me they could leave, or sit over in that booth."

Irene's stomach dropped. What did that mean they weren't there?

Nyke? Maybe warn your brothers?

His hand wrapped protectively around her waist.

Already ahead of you.

"Thanks, Ruby. For everything. We will go see if we can find them."

Ruby gave her a sidelong glance. "It appears to me that maybe you should just take this information and run, Ivy."

Irene wanted to correct her. Tell her who she really was. Hesitation had her opening her mouth with nothing to come out.

"Ivy, you go. The less I know, the better. No one has a squeaky clean past." Her eyes turned on Nyke. "You take care of this girl. I don't care what happened in the past, you treat her right."

A grunt was all Nyke said as he pulled her away.

A pang of regret or possibly concern wouldn't go away. Saying goodbye hadn't gotten rid of the issue. That wasn't how it was supposed to be. Saying goodbye was closure. Irene should have felt fine. She should have been okay. Everything should have aligned and the world should have made sense. Or, well, maybe not the whole world. Her father still existed and coming back here was a reminder.

My brother's said some strange men exited a few moments before we walked in.

She breathed out a sigh of relief. *So they left?*

Nyke flexed his neck before answering and paused at the back door. *I didn't say that.*

Oh God. Clutching the wall, she tried to keep herself standing as the lights appeared to flicker above them.

Nyke? Are my eyes messing with me?

He turned to her and spiked her fear with his one quick shake of the head.

Nyke pushed through the back door into dead silence. Strange for a city where the sirens never seemed to stop.

Stay behind me. Nyke said.

It was then that Irene realized the alley was crawling. The brick slithered in reflection of the moon.

My father. Was all she could say as her throat tightened against a scream.

y? Barak? Where are you? Eadric, get out of here.

Cy and Barak stormed through the door, pausing one by one as their eyes focused on the shit-show in front of them. Nyke looked at his brothers, their eyes glowing eerily in the dark, and the scales lining their skin glinted. All the lights in the alley were out leaving the moon to do what it does best. Cast shadows and hide the shit that goes bump in the night.

Great.

Nyke? Eadric asked through the connection.

You gone yet? Nyke asked.

Duck, was all Eadric said as a flash of white fire blasted against one wall.

The three of them turned and hunkered down in half human, half dragon form. Nyke's body wrapped around Irene.

A sick, unearthly hissing filled the dead night.

They turned to see what had just happened as a heat seemed to fill the alley way.

Eadric walked up beside them and jerked his head to the side. Nyke's eyes were drawn to a familiar female as she slowly followed the white flame forward.

You allowed your mate to stay?

Their job was to protect their females, and here Eadric was okay letting her fight.

Eadric shrugged. *I couldn't stop her. Besides, this is what she is made for. Her words not mine.*

The hisses gave way to shrieks until the one side was quiet. Nyke whipped around, a new chittering sound behind them.

"Is that Lilly?" asked Irene, her eyes saucers.

Nyke wanted to answer her, but he forced her around to see what he saw.

"Recognize any of these?"

Her fear seeped into him through their connection. He had no choice; he needed to see what she knew and invaded her mind.

It took Nyke a few seconds to grip what he saw. Her mind was dark. But it wasn't for lack of her thinking.

No, she was in a dark room. The same chittering sound on the walls. Irene frozen, similar to how she was right now. She was terrified in her mind. Nyke didn't like this at all.

He watched her in this memory.

He could see her heat signature thanks to his dragon's eyes, but otherwise this room was dark, and she was blind here. She held out her hands and cried in the memory. Nyke wanted to reach out and hold her, but this was just a memory, nothing more.

Seconds passed in her memory and she jumped ahead to what came next. One creature after another attacked her, biting her. The only light in her dream was the strange heat where her hands touched each creature.

They stopped and disappeared, or at least he assumed they did. The creatures didn't have any heat. They didn't have a heartbeat. They smelled rotten and dead. Slowly they stopped approaching. He could hear their chittering fade off towards the walls again.

As she screamed over and over, and over he backed out of her mind.

Irene stood, sheet white, frozen to the ground. He held her tightly as his brothers separated down the alley.

"Irene, do not be afraid. You aren't alone this time," he said.

She shook. "My father knew I didn't have any powers. Or at least he knew I didn't have much for power. But he put me in the room, anyway. Without Lilly." Her voice quivered on her sister's name.

"How do we kill them?"

Irene gripped his forearm. "I don't know. My sister's fire is a given. It's demonic in nature. I seemed to be able to release them from whatever those shells are, but then they find a new body to inhabit. In that training room they were bound to that space, and there were no other bodies. Here though, in a city this big? There are too many choices."

Irene flinched as something launched itself toward her. Nyke's hand shot out, gripping the creature.

"Duck," hollered Eadric.

The thing squealed and shook in his hand.

Nyke turned to look at the charred skeleton in his hand.

"Thanks," he said.

Eadric appeared by his side, Lilly in tow.

"There are too many of them and Lilly can't keep track of all of them."

"I'm sorry. These things are my father's favorite game. They regenerate faster than I can kill them. Irene, are you okay?"

Nyke allowed Lilly through as she grabbed onto Irene's hands. His mate was shaking, and he didn't know what to think or do. He couldn't fight a memory. He fucking hated feeling powerless. He hated this mission more and more with every passing day.

Irene, are you okay? he asked.

She turned to him, but she stayed attached to her sister.

I don't know.

The chittering and hissing suddenly stopped.

That wasn't a good sign. Nyke and the others slowly turned, watching as the walls stilled before the eerie voices spoke in unison, a snake's tongue dragging over every s.

"We will alwaysss find you. You can't hide. Come home," the voices said.

Nyke shivered at the words. No, he didn't. His mates fear pulsed through him in a strangling string of icy fear. Fuck.

He reached out and grabbed Irene. Screw her sister, or the creatures.

"Irene, look at me." His hands gripped her upper arms. He wanted to shake the fear from her but he knew it wouldn't work.

Instead, he claimed her lips. Pressing her ice cold lips to answer to the heat of his touch. He pressed her to open for him.

His magic curved itself around her like a blanket. It would heal her, his heat would protect her.

She answered his touch, and slowly her body thawed under his grip. Her lips moved with his and she began to breathe.

The kiss lasted seconds, but in those few seconds he could feel the life within her shift. Something in her snapped.

He pulled away as light flashed behind him and a massive shape of one of his brother's dragons ripped through the night.

"I need to leave you for a moment. Stay close to your sister."

She blinked at him. He didn't have time to wait. Nyke gave her a chaste kiss before turning.

Stop, Nyke. We can't win.

He snarled at her words and shifted.

The space was tight, but their dragons didn't mind as their claws sunk into the brick of the walls, impaling creatures while their jaws tore at others. The inky taste of rot filled his beast.

Nyke, stop. Stop.

He didn't. His brothers continued to fight the onslaught as the opening to the alley continued to darken and the walls refilled with creatures.

Fuck. We aren't even making a dent. Maybe we just leave and they will disappear?

Came Eadric's voice.

More white flashes of light, Lilly, he assumed.

Irene? You're okay?

Fuck. She didn't answer, but he knew she was alive or he'd have felt it.

He breathed out a breath of fire, setting the things ablaze and marking them. It was easier to find something lit like a torch. They ran and skittered, adding light to the dark space.

His brothers ripped away groups of the things and yet more continued.

I think we've worn out our welcome. Nyke said, seeing no way out of this and winning.

Irene, we are leaving.

She didn't answer him as he backed up to where he'd just left her.

Where was she? He turned in a circle, whipping his head one way then the next. His heart stopped at a scream. He shifted between dragon and human, his hands still clawed and his skin still scaled.

"Stop!" Irene shouted again.

She ran past him, his arms shooting out to stop her. She fought him, though. "Let me go. Let me do this."

Irene, calm yourself. Stop.

Her mind was a mix of anger and fear and revenge.

Nyke wouldn't allow this to cloud her judgment, only he didn't have much choice as she grabbed his claw and bit down.

It didn't hurt, but damn if it didn't surprise the hell out of him.

Let me go. No matter what I do, don't follow. Not yet.

He released her, apprehension filling the space in his chest. What was she going to do?

It was then that Nyke realized the entire alley was quiet. The only sound was Lilly screaming. How had he missed her? Nyke glimpsed Eadric holding her back as her hair flew around her wildly.

"No. Irene. Stop," Lilly repeated over and over.

What was Irene going to do?

"Stop her. She can't. Stop her," Lilly screamed. She finally stopped fighting Eadric Her eyes burning into Nyke's. "She's going back to him. She won't survive if she does."

Nyke didn't even wait for the last words to leave Lilly's mouth as he turned with lightning speed to stop his mate. She was only a few feet in front of him. He would catch her and fly away. She wouldn't do this to him. She wouldn't do this to her sister. She wouldn't do this to herself.

The creatures converged on Irene faster than his steps could move.

Fuck it. He lunged forward trying to catch her, but all his arms caught was air.

I love you.

The last words echoing through his brain as everything in the alley disappeared and the silence of the world disappeared.

Irene? Irene, where are you?

Nothing.

He pounded his fists into the ground. It was solid. Where was she? She couldn't have just disappeared into thin air.

Footsteps thundered against the ground.

"Irene? No. She went back. She went back," Lilly cried out.

Nyke looked back as he watched Eadric wrap her in his arms.

"Where is she? Where did she go?" he growled.

Eadric shot him a look, but he didn't fucking care. He sprang to his feet and stormed over to Lilly.

"Where did she go? Where did those things take her?"

Lilly swallowed a sob and looked at him.

"She went back to my father. Those things, they answer to him. They are one of his tests."

Nyke knew what she was talking about. He'd seen the memory. "Why would he send them? How did they take her?"

Lilly shrugged. "That's what they do. They disappear when they have what they want and reappear to my dad. I've seen it happen. My father never does his own work, even I knew that, and I was locked away most of my life."

Nyke roared into the night. He tried to trace her scent, but it didn't go any further than the one spot. She'd just vanished.

"Where do we look?" he started to scream at Lilly.

Eadric let her go and pushed against his chest.

"Calm down. We will find her."

"How? How do we find her if no one knows where to look? Ask her. Ask your mate, where do we go?"

Nyke's throat constricted as the fear within him surfaced. He always had a plan. He always knew what was next. He stood up, lost. Where was he supposed to go?

He tried to calm himself, let his dragon's senses take over. His hands shook.

Could he find her? He should be able to sense her.

The world faded away. He needed to find her. Instinct took over. He started to walk, but his dragon snarled at the too slow pace. No, they would take to the sky.

"Nyke, stop. We will go with you. Wait."

He didn't bother waiting or listening. He shifted, and he didn't give a damn who saw him as he moved to the street to take off.

In the back of his mind he could feel his brothers, but right now he didn't care if they kept up or not. He was lost in his need to find his mate. He needed a plan and the best he could come up with was to trace his bond. His heart would lead him, and if it didn't, he would die trying to find her.

17

*I*rene backed into the corner, keeping her eyes closed. Her heart panicked enough without seeing what she'd just done. She was not opening her eyes. Not yet.

No. She wouldn't do that. Not until she was certain those things were gone. She hated those creatures, but something she'd learned is they couldn't hurt her. She wasn't sure why, but the worst of them was the fear. Her father didn't know that, though. And that was for the best. He used anything he saw of value. She didn't want to be used anymore.

Irene listened, realizing the sounds had stopped. Smelling the air, visions of her past sat front and center in her mind. A familiar scent of bleach. For as evil an ass as her father was, he hated germs, or perhaps it was he hated the smell of suffering.

She paused as she realized she was picking up much more than bleach. She could hear every detail from the air circulating to buzzing of lights. She'd never noticed that before. Maybe Nyke's powers were still with her, even if she had just left him.

She gulped at the air as the sting of pain throbbed in her chest. Would he ever forgive her if she didn't make it out of here alive? A tear threatened to surface, one more reason not to open her eyes. She needed to block out the sadness, no heartbreak. She needed to get through this first and then, when she'd ensured that she wasn't leaving her father to hurt more and more creatures, she would return to Nyke. If he would take her back.

Her hand traced her lips, the memory of their last kiss. She needed to shake this from her head. Irene needed to focus. The difference this time is even without her sister here, she still had everything to lose. She couldn't have done this when it was just her, alone with no one to risk. Why would she succeed now?

Nyke?

There was nothing. He wasn't in her head. This shouldn't have been that hard, she'd been alone most of her life. The emptiness now though, seemed cavernous.

Irene focused on her surroundings again. A shift of fabric caught her attention. Someone was here?

"Daughter? You're home now."

Her skin prickled at the sound. Slowly, she opened her eyes and turned her head. There he was. In the corner on a stool. The white room familiar to how she'd lived previously.

"Perhaps you can enlighten me as to why you allowed yourself to be found with those lizards."

Her mouth opened and closed. What was she supposed to say? What was the right answer?

"I don't blame you, child. You returned willingly, my pets have assured me of that."

God, his voice. It instilled a healthy dose of fear. She didn't want to go back to being one of his experiments anymore than she wanted to be punished for leaving him.

"I did. I returned by choice. They kidnapped me when Lilly left. Surely you saw this on the cameras."

He folded his long, boney fingers in his lap.

"Alas, no. Your sister destroyed everything on that mountain. Do you have any idea how hard it is to rebuild an army?"

She nearly scoffed, but swallowed it instead.

"I can't say I do," she said.

He scowled. "Well, let's not worry. At least I have one more now that you have returned. Do you have anything helpful for me?"

That was it? Of course it was. He was heartless. Looking at him, having seen humans in the real world, Irene questioned if he was even really human.

Right now, she was in a sticky spot. She wasn't bullet proof or demon proof. She wasn't immune to her father. She couldn't go through those treatments again.

Why had she come back? She was starting to question the logic. Her only thought was she needed the attack to stop, the creatures to go away, to keep her sister and Nyke safe.

She'd thought maybe coming back she could get rid of her father. Sitting in the cold white space, looking into eyes that had no other description than dead, she wasn't so sure she could do anything.

Breathe. She could do this. She wasn't alone anymore. She'd been loved. No, she was loved. He would come for her no matter what she'd said. There was no doubt in her mind. But she was going to end this asshole before they went home. She couldn't leave him here to hurt more innocent people and creatures.

Irene knew now why she'd come back. Yes, she'd wanted to save those she loved because it was a beautiful feeling to feel. But this was for her. She couldn't live the rest of her life knowing what she knew. The nightmares would haunt her.

"Yes, I have something for you."

She stood tall and pushed away from the wall. "You wanted dragon DNA, and I saw no other way to do this than to get them to trust me."

Her father shifted, enough that she was at least positive the man was living. "I'm listening."

"What were your plans for the DNA?" she asked, as if she didn't know the answer.

He nodded. "As one of my scientists, I'm certain you would understand when I say I would make us an ultimate weapon. That kind of discovery would secure our place in this world."

Irene nodded. "Yes, but don't you already have demons at your beck and call?"

Her father steepled his hands. "Hmm. Yes, but you of all people should know that you don't stop. Besides, even demons can be stopped. Perhaps not by someone like you, but well. Yes. Let's just call it diversification."

She tipped her head. "For what?"

He tipped a hand to her. "Power. For power."

She blinked and almost missed a subtle nod of his head.

"Oh. Okay. And you think you could create something strong with their DNA?"

"Well, daughter. I suppose my answer depends on what you have brought me."

She swallowed. What she was about to say could either sink her or save her.

"Your experiments, before I left, were trying to infuse my body with demonic matter. You were trying to prepare me to carry a child, I wasn't blind to your processes."

He might as well have rolled his eyes, although all he did was raise his brow.

"Well, I didn't exactly have a good way to collect their DNA. But you promise me that I will be protected as well as what I am about to say."

He stood, slowly. "I have no reason to doubt you, child. Those that are loyal are always protected."

Filling her lungs, she breathed out a long steadying breath.

"I'm pregnant, and the child is one of theirs."

Irene paused and waited.

"You are certain?" he asked.

Irene slipped back into her new self at his dumb comment.

"Really? Am I sure of what? It's theirs or that I'm pregnant? I have zero reason to lie."

Her father was not amused. "No need to be ill mannered. Is this what the outside world does to obedient children? Perhaps we should be relieved that we found you when we did."

She shuddered.

"Father, the outside world isn't easy. One adapts to survive. I'm sure you can understand. Where are we anyway?"

His eyes flashed to a dark black, something she'd learned to expect from possessed shells of humans, but with her father he was in control of it. Being away from all this, from him, she now wondered what exactly her father was that he looked neither human nor demon. For years she assumed he was human, that this was all normal. But the guards, they were possessed by her father's minions or blinded by the power her father promised them.

The humans on the outside, they didn't look like them. They were free. They were normal. She should have noticed the creature in the club for what it was. Instead, she'd only seen what she wanted to see.

None of this helped her feel like she knew what to do to kill him though.

"After your sister's betrayal, we had to move yet again. I'm running low on my patience with her. She's been brainwashed by those creatures. We are in a large area of abandoned buildings. Perhaps you were not here when we captured one of them? Certainly this place has allowed us more opportunities to observe these magnificent creatures. You'd have been no use to them of course. I can see why you would be left behind."

She clenched her jaw. She was so tired of being told she was useless. She wanted to tell him he was wrong. She'd saved the very creatures he'd tried to control from the start. But, no. That wouldn't do her any good. She didn't want to be seen as a threat. She needed access to him.

"Oh. Okay. No. I didn't know you had captured one of them."

Secretly, she hoped Nyke would come here. Find her, but she needed time to figure out what to do first. She needed to understand her father's weakness if he had one.

"Of course you didn't. Perhaps, now though you may be the one of use to me."

She didn't have enough patience to be upset by his sharp tongue. She knew what he thought of her. It fueled her anger.

Irene placed her hand over her stomach. She wasn't sure that she was pregnant, to be honest. She knew her father would push for tests, but she might buy some time for herself at least. Besides, there was a good enough chance she could be pregnant thanks to the drugs her father injected her with. Right now she wouldn't hate that, it would be a comfort to have a part of her dragon. She needed to be strong, and as much as she tried, she wasn't sure if she could be strong on her own.

Irene focused on her breathing. She tried to contact Nyke again. She'd told him not to stop her, to not come after her. But the longer she was away from him, the more she wanted to reassure herself that he would come when she was ready.

He would. If only she could tell him where to go.

"Daughter, I suppose we should find you a place more comfortable than this room. For your sake, I hope you have better luck than your mother."

Irene tried to think back on her own mother. The blank spaces in her mind clouded her memories, though. A sharp pain shot through her brain and she winced, her hands flying to her temples. Her father's words seemed muffled as the pain cleared her head. She needed to know what these blank spots were. She needed to know what she couldn't remember. Perhaps that was the key to getting rid of her father?

"I will notify our new doctor of your condition. Come, I'll

take you to a room. The greater good always has a price, I'm quite proud that you have been willing to sacrifice yourself. Very promising indeed," her father seemed to mumble to himself as they walked out.

Holding herself, she tried to fight against the chill seeping in.

Irene walked down the corridor, trying to keep her eyes down. She didn't want to look. Didn't want to see that she was right back where she didn't want to be.

This place was strange, not the same at least. Not nearly as nice as the lab, but it also had a strange energy around it. Much different from that of the labs. Irene wondered if she could reach out and grab her father and do what she did to all his victims. The fear that he had no soul resurfaced.

The idea of touching him had her stomach churning.

Memories of how she'd helped Nyke, though, how she'd pushed out the demon magic, joined in her endless thoughts and questions. Perhaps she could do that? Her father definitely would have demon magic. Seeing how he controlled so many of them and how in recent years, all his experiments had turned to demon energy exchanges rather than strictly shifters and aliens made it seem even more likely.

She shuffled behind him, unsure if the sour turn of her stomach was nerves or her lie manifesting. What if she really was pregnant? Her body heated in anger, a fire lighting within her. There was no way she'd let him use her baby. And if she wasn't, there was no way she'd do anything her father wanted either.

Had he ever been human? Was he still human, but one more experiment gone wrong?

As they walked she tried to remember her mother again. She could get a clear picture of a woman stuck in a small cell just like her sister. She had some things though, and Irene had been allowed to visit. How could she remember so little? Her mother had been around for years. Or at least long enough to be remembered.

Going back into her memories again, she tried to pick at the corners of her mind that seemed like they had a secret she just had to unlock. She pushed harder, this time she could ignore the pain.

A thought struck her as she wondered if her father had ever made any other children successfully from his experiments?

She would have met them, wouldn't she?

"Father?"

He walked at a steady pace in silence. She feared he wasn't going to answer her.

"Yes?" he finally responded as he stopped by a door.

"Were Lilly and I your only children."

He turned to face her, his eyes more creepy black than human. Fear coiled within her stomach. She wasn't sure if she preferred his near gray, colorless iris to the black. They both made it hard to look at him.

"You are my only child. Now, your room. The doctor will come tend to you when he has time. I have places to be."

He reached for the doorknob, but didn't walk her in. Not surprising, but she wanted to see if she could brush against his skin and see what happened. Maybe.

The idea scared her.

Breathing out, she shook her head. Here goes nothing, she thought.

She held out her hand. "Thank you, father for welcoming me back."

He glared at her hand.

"Yes, well. I am pleased you have seen the light for the greater good."

He went to turn around and Irene took another risk; she reached for his hand as he turned. Instantly a bout of nausea hit her, forcing her to let go.

Irene pushed open the bedroom door and looked around for the bathroom.

No, he wasn't human. Not even a little. She needed to unlock her memories and fast. She needed out, but something in her mind told her she needed this last piece of information.

*N*yke scoured the skies. He would get so far and then the trail would disappear. There was something blocking her and he was damn near ready to just start burning every building in his path.

Cy came up next to him, his wings gliding alongside him. Nyke banked with the current and tried to chase off Cy or any of his brothers. Instead, they corrected themselves and stayed with him.

He didn't want them. He wanted his mate. His Irene. What the hell had she been thinking? Why would she leave him?

It's a dead end brother, said Cy.

His dragon snapped at the air.

Not a dead end. We wait. She will contact me. She did this for me, for us. We do not abandon my mate. Never.

Cy's dragon huffed, but he remained steadfast.

Eadric? Has Lilly thought of anything that would help us?

There had to be more to the sisters. There was something dark in Irene's memories. He could feel the absence of something, and maybe Lilly was the key to unlocking it.

Nothing. She said she has similar memories of the demons and then nothing.

Nyke snarled and banked again.

We aren't far from where Deo was held captive. Perhaps we fly there for now? Cy said.

Finally, something that was helpful. Not that Nyke didn't think this doctor would have remained in the same place for long, but there were few options. Perhaps instead of expecting the expected, they needed to go with what seemed out of character. The doctor was cocky. He might have remained at those underground labs had it not been for their destruction of the facilities.

Fine. But this time we go in under the radar. No more obvious attacks.

Cy's dragon grinned.

That's the old Nyke. Let's go.

Maybe as they flew, he would pick up on her magic, their connection, anything. Maybe Lilly would have some breakthrough. Eadric said she was just as stressed out. He doubted that. This was his mate. His soul. She'd allowed herself to go back to the place she hated most in all the world. Fuck, he hated it and she'd only shared some of her memories.

Lead the way and pray to the goddess Irene is there.

He didn't add that if she wasn't, there would be hell to pay. Literally. He would find a way to hell and slaughter ever fucking demon until he got his answer.

Nyke's dragon stretched his long neck as something strong and magical hit him. They sniffed the air and glided over old mills of some kind. There were too many buildings, but something was here.

They stayed high above the clouds, taking in the sites below between the breaks in their finicky hiding spot. So many metal buildings, some with cracked and dirty windows. All scented of decay and rust. Nyke dove closer and sniffed the air.

There was a fine line between the fresh air and something else. The sour, acrid scent that had surrounded Deo.

Did you smell that, Cy?

The other dragon dipped below the clouds, coming back up seconds later.

Yes. It's the same scent that covered Deo. Took him days to clean himself up.

Nyke might have laughed, except he wasn't in the mood.

Do you think that means he's still here?

Cy nodded.

He hung back and circled back. *Let's head for the ground, back there.*

Cy followed and as they neared the ground they each shifted, dropping a few feet in the air. They had no time to waste, that was the only certainty.

Both Cy and Nyke stopped and glared at a metal gate that leaned as if it had tired of waiting for someone to care again.

Nyke was tired of waiting. Perhaps he and the fence weren't much different. He smirked.

"What's so funny brother?" asked Cy.

Nyke shot him a glance and kept walking.

"Nothing is funny, perhaps that is what is so funny. I am tired of these doctor's games."

Cy nodded. They were all growing tired of the complications, but Nyke was certain no one was more tired than Nyke. He had yet to even catch a whiff of his mate.

Nyke couldn't worry about that right now. Once his mate was in his possession, he could keep her safe. They could keep moving and avoid this asshole ever finding them again.

How so much evil was allowed in one body, made Nyke truly wonder about Irene and Lilly.

Cy elbowed him out of his thoughts.

There. We can sneak through there. I have not seen any heat signatures of electronics, no cameras.

Slowly and silently they crouched in long grasses as they approached the gaping hole in a fence line. They wouldn't be the first going this way, but Nyke doubted that the doctor would have used such an entrance to get in.

They pressed close to the first building.

Are you getting anything? asked Cy.

Nyke shook his head. It was a wasteland of magic right now. His nose wrinkled at the scent, though. Perhaps if they just followed that scent they would get close enough.

They walked in the shadows the best two males could. Nothing came out for them, yet. Nyke kept watch for cameras. They both looked for wards or magical spells, but there was nothing. Why did nothing with this human work like they expected?

Cy? We are here on Earth for our mates, but what if the goddess designed this all?

Nyke was good at seeing the big picture. Good at finding the hole in the enemy, he had to be. He strategized.

She's done some shitty things to warriors before. I don't know that we can think she didn't send us here for a reason, Cy said.

Really, Nyke knew that their lack of finding mates had been what brought them here. But what if this was some divine design? Fate to end an evil that this planet had yet to see. An evil that they had never seen.

Have you picked up on your mate yet? asked Cy.

Sniffing the air, he still couldn't catch a scent.

Irene?

More nothing.

Nyke listened. Things were much too quiet. No skittering of a rat or tweet of a bird.

His skin shivered, his dragon surfaced, their arms and skin turning to scales. Something had the dragons spooked, and it was best to think with instinct.

As they moved around the rusted metal, Nyke and Cy avoided

heading into any building. Only the goddess knew what was behind door number one, and she wasn't sharing.

Nyke kept reaching for Irene every few feet. She never responded until she did.

His heart stopped. Nyke paused, and Cy nearly ran into him.

What is it?

Nyke couldn't be sure, but he felt something familiar in the air.

She's here. Close.

Nyke looked around. They stood in the middle of a courtyard. A rusted train car and a few sparse patches of weeds, the only things decorating the space.

Shit. We are too exposed.

An inky black thing slithered behind a pane of broken windows.

What was that? asked Cy.

Nyke shook his head. He didn't care, he just wanted Irene right now.

His ears caught breathing. He sniffed the air. He couldn't pick up anything but the sour demon stench.

He motioned to Cy and slipped around the side of the large rusted container. Cy crouched around the other side. At this point they were surrounded if something was good and well watching. The way his skin crawled, something was watching.

Tingles of magic danced along his arms. She was here, so why didn't she answer?

A loud clang echoed throughout the complex.

Cy nodded and without another word they both shifted. Their dragon forms were no less conspicuous at this point than anything else. Something was definitely watching.

Cy hopped up on the metal container at a better vantage point as Nyke circled around the space, waiting for the magic to pull him in the right direction.

He would be chaining her up the second he found her. His

anger kept him sane as he circled back and finally found the threads of magic.

I'll be right back.

Cy nodded. *Hurry. Let's get out of here quickly. I don't like the shadows moving in the buildings.*

Nyke's dragon remained low to ground as he followed the magic. He didn't know why nothing was attacking, but he was going to take it as a gift until proven wrong.

He turned around a corner and sniffed the air again. Licking his lips the dragon had finally found her. She was here somewhere. Something dark passed by more broken and dirty windows.

Quickly, he ate up the distance from where he stood down the tight alley between the buildings. Turning his head one way then the other he watched for her heat signature. And there, up ahead behind a small group of barrels was a tiny figure.

Nyke climbed over one barrel and looked down. The small figure shrieked before she smiled up at him.

"I knew you would come," she said.

His dragon sniffed as he nuzzled her. Fuck it if they didn't have time for this.

Mate, why have you not answered me?

She remained silent. He nuzzled her again.

He couldn't get her to open up and he didn't understand why. For now he needed her out of here.

He looked down and saw the blood on her ankle and realized why her scent had changed. She was covered in the signature black goo and she was bleeding. Still, he'd found her.

He paused a moment.

She's hurt. I'm grabbing her and we go.

Nyke didn't bother waiting for a response. He reached his claw over and grabbed Irene as carefully as he could. She gripped his talon.

He turned around as a loud screech filled the dead silence. And that was a good sign the welcome had been worn out.

Cy's golden hide raced around the corner.

Nyke, let's go.

Without a second word they both pushed off into the sky. Something black and skinny lashed out from one of the windows and grabbed onto Nyke's leg. He shook the thing but it didn't release.

Cy, he said.

His brother answered in seconds as Cy dove in and sprayed fire at the thing. The loud echo of its piercing cry followed as Nyke gained height.

Let's get out of here.

Nyke nodded, but not before he looked back and saw several more tentacles climbing out of a window. In fact, he noticed that most of the windows darkened.

Anger surfaced. Now that his mate was safe, the only thing left was blinding rage. He would not leave without making a statement.

Dipping low enough, but not too low, he allowed his fire to fill him. As he reached the center of the darkening buildings, he let his fire out. It sprayed over too many dark figures to know exactly how many or what he'd hit, but he would allow the images to bring him satisfaction as he continued ahead without looking back. They were headed back home.

Irene stared at the wall, a blanket wrapped around her. Hours in that place and she'd nearly lost her mind. Had it really only been hours before she'd lost all sense? How had she survived years with her father?

The magic was off the charts darkness. There were fewer flesh and blood guards, and for once that had been an advantage. She'd been able to wander without anyone questioning her. Everything she'd found circled in her head.

Irene played the scene repeatedly. Walking down the hall until she found a lab. She'd nearly forgotten her fear of her father, his labs, being discovered. All she wanted was to get to a computer.

She hadn't been prepared for what was there, though. One file after another about failed experiments. A new species of alien incompatible with a substance he called D2020.

One folder buried deep in another file caught her attention. It needed a password, different from most of the others. It had taken her far too long to break the code, but lucky for her she'd been on the wrong side of all this for years and this file was old.

The moment she'd opened it, something flooded through her.

"Irene? Are you okay?"

Irene gasped in surprise as Lilly placed her hand on her shoulder. Oh right. She wasn't there anymore. She was here, on a spaceship. Her mate had left her to get something warm to drink, but only after she begged him to go. Lilly must have been his compromise. It was fine; she was a part of this.

How did she tell her sister any of this information? She said the first thing in her mind, the first of her own clues that something had been wrong.

"I, I don't know. Have you ever tried to think of our mother?" Irene asked.

Lilly shrugged. "No. I mean, yes. The only memories I have are the day I - I mean the day she died."

Irene placed her hand over her sisters. She knew Lilly blamed herself. She had indirectly caused her mother to die, but knowing her father, it had all been designed perfectly. And the design had been to ensure his hands stayed clean.

"It's okay, Lilly, I think he designed it that way."

Her sister sat down next to her on the bench in what Irene was starting to nickname the hub. It was more of a common area where everyone seemed to be. She'd wanted to be alone, but after being looked over, Nyke wouldn't allow it. Or rather, he wouldn't let her be without him and he'd needed to be with his brothers.

The minutes ticked by and Irene gave in. She needed to tell him what she'd seen, anyway. They all needed to know.

First, she needed to tell Lilly though.

Irene glanced out of the corner of her eye as Nyke slammed a fist down on a table.

He was pissed off, and she understood, sort of. She let a small smile tug at the corner of her lips. He cared about her so much that what had happened pissed him off. He wanted revenge, but didn't they all? What she knew now might change the course of everything. Maybe

"Can't you read Nyke's mind. Tell me what's going on over there?" Lilly asked.

Irene shrugged. "I can, when I focus. But right now, well. My head is spinning."

What could she say? Irene had run through a lot of scenarios.

How could she tell everyone that Lilly and Irene were products of their father's second failures? Irene swallowed. She couldn't unsee the truth.

She also wasn't positive that the information would change everything. Irene believed it would, but there was nothing predictable with her father.

Irene couldn't think of Lilly as anything but fragile. Or, well, maybe not fragile. She looked healthy and happy, now. But Irene couldn't unsee her as her baby sister that needed protecting. The one she watched out for. The small frail kid everyone feared.

"Lilly, you're happy here, right?"

Her sister smiled. "I never knew happiness like this existed. I never realized there was something to wake up for that didn't involve fearing for your safety." She giggled.

"I agree with you, that this is what I never knew I always craved. But what if I told you that there was something else out there? Someone else. Someone that we need to find regardless of what we want?"

Lilly stood up and backed away. "Irene, no. I am not going back to father. How could you even think that?"

The room went silent and Irene scrambled. As quick as her sister had stood she tried to spit out her next words. "No. Not father. Another sister."

She didn't need their mates to panic. They were already on edge.

The wide-eyed look Lilly gave her said it all.

"There's what?" asked Lilly.

She slowed down. "Another sister. We have an older sister and

I think she can stop father, forever. I think he made us forget her somehow. Messed with our minds."

Irene tried to sink further down in her blanket as every eye in the room settled on her.

"What do you mean there's another sister?" Nyke said, coming to her.

Her stomach flipped at the sight of her warrior. Her soul had missed him. She'd been cold and lonely without him, and she never wanted to feel that way again. She also knew that he and everyone else in the room couldn't rest with her father out there.

Nyke knelt in front of her. "There is a third? Why didn't you say so? We would have gone back for her."

He pushed back a strand of her hair and the heat of his fingers sent a tingle of longing through her.

Closing her eyes, she allowed the heat of him to calm her nerves.

She isn't there, Nyke.

He nodded as if he knew what she was saying, and maybe he did.

"I think things are clear, that the goddess sent us here for more than just to find our mates."

Maddie and Aisha came to stand with the others. Everyone was there.

Swallowing down her doubt, she needed to get it off her chest.

"I remember her." Irene felt a tear slide down her cheek as she took in the menacing power before her. This is what a family was. It wasn't what her father had tried to create.

"Irene, why are you crying?" Nyke asked, his thumb swiping as more tears overwhelmed her.

"I'm fine. I promise." She sniffled.

"Sis, it will be okay. I promise," said Lilly.

She wanted to know when her fragile little sister had grown up so much. More tears threatened as she realized that she not only got a chance at happiness, and a family, she got to see her sister grow up now.

"No. It isn't that. For once in my life, I know it will be okay. I never thought I'd ever feel that. I suddenly understand how Lilly could walk back into father's lab with confidence. I thought you were crazy. But, I get it."

"Then why are you crying?" asked Lilly.

Irene pursed her lips. "Our sister, I remember why we can't remember her. I remember that night, or well a night. You were locked in your room like always," she said, looking at her sister. "I was supposed to be in bed, but I couldn't sleep. I was going to sneak down the hall to her room. Only, I heard her and father fighting. Or rather, he was threatening her. I remember seeing a dark shadow move into her room, but I didn't realize what it was."

No one spoke. Everyone was staring at her. Well, if she didn't feel like a freak before all this, she did right now.

"Irene, I can feel you. No one is judging, but if this can help us we need to know."

She paused. "I think she's the missing piece we need to stop my father. Whatever she did that night had him scared. Nothing ever had him scared. There was a bright light and then nothing. He walked out of her room screaming at someone or something. Guards started running to the stairs. When I finally got to her room, it was empty. She had just disappeared."

Lilly shook her head. "Did we not remember because she died? Maybe it was stress? I would prefer to remember fewer people dying."

Irene shifted. "No. It wasn't stress. It was him. He manipulated us and until I saw the file again, anything I tried to remember just hurt. But once I saw the facts, the truth on her. Well, she's alive. Or they believe she is and she can create something, portals. Her name is Skylar."

If Irene had ever wondered how to kill a conversation, this

had been it. No one spoke. Not her sister, not the other mates. None of the dragons.

"I thought, maybe we should figure out how to track her?" Irene hoped they agreed, and that she wasn't just sending all of them on another chase. Worse, what if finding her was a trap? What if her leaving without ever coming back was a sign and they shouldn't ignore it?

One by one, each of the men looked at each other. Perhaps they were having a conversation where she couldn't hear.

"Could we be a part of this?" Irene asked. Now she was just getting angry. "I just risked my life by going back there to get this information. I think I should be involved in a plan."

Nyke nodded. "We will need some more ideas of where to look for her? Without any idea, this will be like looking for a single blade of grass in a meadow."

Irene nodded. "I think I can help with that. I just need some time. Perhaps Lilly can help me?"

Lilly shrugged. "Whatever you need, I am here."

The air didn't seem as cold anymore, and she dropped the blanket. Having a plan seemed to help her feel a little better. A new hope blossoming in her chest. The dread that had sat like a rock in her stomach had seemed to have worn away and she could breathe.

Things would be okay, they just needed to find their missing link. She had some ideas in her head as to how they might all work together.

Had her father not been a giant asshole, there was a chance he might have created the ultimate weapon. Little did he know that weapon was going to destroy him.

* * *

She wasn't clear how much time had passed when she couldn't fight back a yawn.

152

"Mate, let's get you to bed. You can explain what the hell happened back there later."

He wrapped his arms around her and pulled her up.

"Wait, Irene? How did you get away this time? Or I mean, how did you get back in with dad? You said you could get to a computer. How?" Lilly asked.

Irene swallowed. She didn't want to do this here, but with nine sets of eyes on her, she felt like she needed to say something.

"I, uh. I said I returned on my own."

Lilly gave Irene a sidelong glance. "And daddy dearest, just let you waltz right in. No questions asked?"

Irene nibbled on the inside of lip. Exactly what she had told her father ran through her mind. What did she say here and now? How could she say it in front of everyone? More though, what could she say right now without creating some crazy panic?

She didn't even know if any of what she had told her father was true. She'd literally left before the test had come back. Why? She remembered why, all two of them.

If she was pregnant, she didn't want to let her father have access to her child and if she wasn't, well; she was afraid her luck may run out. She'd gotten what she needed about her sister. And then she'd got the hell out of there.

She went to open her mouth and froze as she saw Nyke's eyes. Wide-eyed surprise? Maybe it was panic? Oh, shit. He'd been listening in her head.

Before another word escaped her lips, Nyke had her in his arms and was carrying her off.

"Wait, I wanted to hear the rest of the story," she heard Lilly yell down the hall.

"Later," he shouted back.

The whoosh of the door, the only noise breaking through the unnatural silence of Nyke.

He gently put her down on the bed and pinned her in his

gaze. He paced the room for several more seconds. She opened her mouth and closed it multiple times. He'd been listening in on her thoughts. This was his fault. He shouldn't have been spying,* she thought.

"I wasn't spying. I was trying to be there for my mate."

She jumped at his voice.

"How, how is listening being there for me?" she spat back.

He growled. "You are my mate. We have no secrets. If you feel the need to keep secrets I don't see how we will work. That's not what the mating bond is meant to be. You've done nothing but hide things from me. But this."

His words took the air out of her lungs. She'd been single minded for so long, that even through it all with Nyke by her side, she'd never really understood what being part of a team, being a mate meant.

"I'm sorry," she said.

He stopped pulling his hair and turned to look at her. Her body heated under his gaze. The way he looked at her, like he was only truly seeing her now, chased a shiver over her.

"A baby?" he asked.

She picked at her nails before meeting his gaze head on.

"I, I don't know. My father had given me hormone treatments before I escaped. I mean, there was other stuff too, but he was preparing me for another experiment the day Lilly walked back into the lab. And, I. There's something different about my magic. It's not you either. I can feel something different in me."

Nyke's tight lipped expression changed, slowly sliding into a smile as he came to kneel before her.

"Promise me to stop hiding things from me? I want to keep you safe," he said.

A fear that she would fail him tried to slither its way into her, but as his hands feathered over her arms, she let the energy of him run over. She could feel the tattoos, his markings heating as she allowed him to comfort her. She nodded her head, finally.

"Fine. No more secrets then. Starting now. I want to go look for my sister. Now," she said.

Nyke didn't speak for far too long and the silence made her nervous.

"Yes. We will. It appears the goddess has destined us to finish this."

His words rolled over her and a sprinkle of hope filled her and something else too. "Wouldn't it be funny if all along she, my sister, had been made for Cy? Is that even possible?"

The warmth of Nyke's lips pressed against her temple. "At this point I don't think anything is funny or accidental. The goddess has a design that none of us understand."

The way his eyes watched her had her squirming.

"And Barak? He has his mate? All this means that soon we can leave?" she asked.

Nyke sighed. "The woman, the one that Deo found. She is apparently Barak's mate. The problem with her is whatever your father did isn't making her very accommodating. Perhaps we go pay her a visit and you work your magic on her? Now, no more distracting me, mate."

Without another word, he pressed forward, claiming her lips. His hunger for her clear. His hands ran over her body as he climbed over her, forcing her to lie down. His lips kissed a trail down the side of her neck as his hand cupped her breast. She moaned, arching into him.

He pulled away for a moment and she couldn't look away.

"I plan to bed you and fill you with my seed until you are positive you are carrying my youngling. And after that I plan to meet your every need for eternity."

She shuddered as his hands dipped below her pants and started to stroke the sensitive bud between her legs.

As she pressed her hips against his skilled fingers, she couldn't help but smile. From this day forward she was not alone, and the idea of giving him a child had her finding a new purpose.

Right after she took down her father.

Maybe.

Nyke's lips claimed hers and she suddenly didn't care what order anything happened.

Nyke's heavy arm wrapped over Irene's body as she shifted. She needed to pee. Slowly she slipped under his arm, trying to keep from disturbing him. Not that she wanted to be in the habit of risking her life, but if last night was any sign of how he would welcome her home, maybe she should.

She winced as she shifted at the soreness of her body. How many times had she come? She wasn't exactly sure.

Padding to the bathroom, she closed the door and stared in the mirror. She stood to the side and envisioned what her body would look like pregnant? The idea had terrified her only a few weeks ago. Her father's idea of children and motherhood wasn't roses and rainbows, though.

Now though, as she ran her hand over her naturally rounder stomach, she was kind of excited. Would Nyke find her sexy, though? She already had too many curves and bumps compared to her sister. He didn't seem to mind though. His hands seemed to love every last curve of her body.

Her hands ran to her breasts as she cupped them. They were slightly sore, and she didn't think that was from Nyke's playful nipping. Maybe it was? She wasn't sure. Wishful thinking?

Turning away from the mirror, she did her thing and then silently left the bathroom.

She yawned as she tried to climb back into bed. Moving his arm, she slid herself back under its heavy weight.

Before she could fall back asleep, he circled his fingers over her belly.

"You smell different, angel."

She squirmed as something large poked her in her rear.

"What does that mean," she asked.

His hand splayed against her skin as she shifted closer.

"It means I believe you may have been right."

Irene swallowed. "Right?"

He chuckled. "My nose doesn't lie. You are with my young."

Her breath hitched. "But we've only been together a few times."

His lips pressed against the back of her head as his chest rumbled.

"Perhaps we've only been together a few days, but in those days I believe I've made up for any lost time since we met."

Realizing she wasn't breathing, she sucked in air. This was okay. This was what you were supposed to do. You were supposed to have babies.

"Mate, why do you now smell of fear?"

She paused next to him. Where did she start? There were a million reasons why. She'd assumed she'd been lying to her father. Sort of. Why had she come up with this plan, anyway? Secretly she'd wanted it? Wanted Nyke's baby. Only those were dreams, and slightly unspoken fears. This was real.

"What if I'm a terrible mother? What if you don't want me anymore?"

He rolled her onto her back and braced himself on top of her. His warm lips kissed a trail from her ear, down her collarbone, over the spot where he'd claimed her, down his markings, over her chest where he stopped to nip at her sensitive nipple. New sensations shot through her at their new sensitivity to damn near everything. He continued his way down, stopping at the sensitive space between her legs. Licking at the bud there, she squirmed.

"What are you doing," she asked breathlessly.

His hands caught up to his trail of kisses where every nerve ending was on fire. His touch running further down her thighs as he spread her legs wide.

"I am showing my mate that you are more sexy to me now than you were when we first met. I can't wait to see your belly round with my youngling and I will prove that to you every day for the rest of your life."

His tongue dipped down between her slit, and she squirmed. Heat was already pooling in her core. Her body already ready for him again. He traced a finger over the sensitive lips down below as he slowly, painfully slowly, pushed his finger inside her.

"Already wet for me, mate?" His voice held a lilt of humor.

"Always ready," she said. Her hips rose to meet his thrust as he slid in a second finger.

Heat coiled within her with each stroke, and he slipped in a third finger as she rocked against him. He knew just where to touch her to make her scream, and it didn't take long for her entire body to quiver under his touch. She was breathless, but still hungry for more. As he rose above her to claim her mouth, she used all her strength to push him over catching him by surprise.

Her body craved him, craved more from him. This time it was her turn to take what she wanted from him at her own pace.

His eyes glinted from human to dragon in the dim lighting as she rose above him, his hands on her hips.

She rubbed her hand between her thighs and brought it back to his length, coating him in her own juices. Slowly, she stretched her muscles as she pushed down onto his rock hard shaft. Her body ached with pleasure with each inch of him she took.

She bit her lower lip to keep herself from crying out.

A moan of his own pleasure filled the silence.

As she seated herself fully over him she paused a moment, loving the feel of how he filled her. Slowly she rocked her hips, rubbing against him with each stroke. It didn't take long for the heat to build again, for the electric need to blind her senses. His hands pushed her forward, harder and faster until there was no option but to give him what he wanted. She broke around him and came for him. Her body taking all the pleasure it wanted.

Irene couldn't catch her breath as his own need grew, and within a second he had her pinned under him as he pounded into her. A few more strokes and she felt the pulsing of him within her. The sensation of him spilling himself deep in her core brought her body to pleasure again. She cried out, taken by surprise. He collapsed onto her, rolling to the side as their hearts beat in a frantic race.

"You are the sexiest female alive," he said, pulling her in closer.

* * *

Space Dragons Seek Mates
Book 1: Must Love Dragons
Book 2: Single Red Dragon
Book 2.5 Dragons Under the Mistletoe
Book 3: Dragon Wanted
Book 4: Looking for a Good Dragon
Book 5: No Scales Needed
Book 6: Desperately Seeking Dragon

ABOUT THE AUTHOR

Michelle's imagination started spilling out onto paper the second she could scribble. Her drawing never improved, but her love affair with words continued and evolved as she became infatuated with one story after another. If life could be written, Michelle would write everyone's ending as a happily ever after.

Michelle grew up in Chicago and later moved to Colorado. Her husband still makes fun of her Midwest accent. She has traded in her engineering degree to raise two little humans and three dogs, and prays she survives it all. Her sanity survives on the pages she writes. As Michelle always says, in a world of serious she writes an escape.

Website: http://www.michellezieglerauthor.com
Newsletter: http://michellezieglerauthor.com/contact/

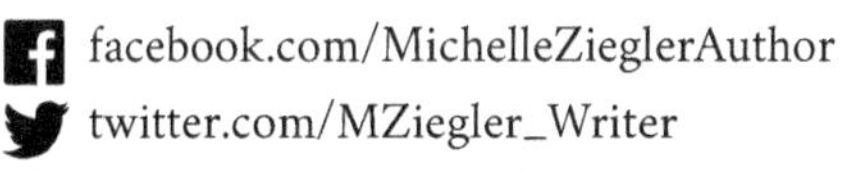

facebook.com/MichelleZieglerAuthor
twitter.com/MZiegler_Writer
instagram.com/mziegler_writer

www.ingramcontent.com/pod-product-compliance
Lightning Source LLC
Chambersburg PA
CBHW061531120726
48001CB00004B/1479